A Lady I Met at Closing Time
and Other Stories

A Lady I Met at Closing Time and Other Stories

Jeffrey Stone

ISBN: **978-0-6152-1983-7**

Library of Congress Control Number: 2008905223

Lulu.com
860 Aviation Pkwy Ste 300
Morrisville NC 27560

A little lie can save a lot of explanation.

Author Unknown

Contents

Preface

There are no superheroes in the stories you are about to read; the truth is, there are no heroes at all. These are tales about ordinary people living ordinary lives with successes and failures, loves and losses, laughter and disappointments. They are imperfect people, but they have their hopes and dreams, and their hearts can be broken and mended—these are the things about which a good story can be told. I have appointed myself to tell these tales because I, like my characters, am ordinary and imperfect, and I am unapologetically incapable of keeping a secret.

If you are at all like me, you are skeptical when an author tells you, or a caption streams across a movie screen to declare, that *this story is based on true events*. For that reason, I have made no such assertion here. I considered telling my readers that the stories contain almost nothing but the truth, but I would have been terribly embarrassed to make that claim when I know that I have taken many liberties in weaving these tales. In fact, as you will undoubtedly discern, I have lied about my characters in a few instances. (Sometimes, a little lie is essential to good story telling. I understand this tradition dates all the way back to Homer.)

It is true that real people in my life planted the kernels that grew into the stories contained here. They span a thirty-year period from adolescence to midlife, including time spent wondering where in the hell all the years went. "Age of Wisdom" starts the volume with its depiction of a country boy stepping through the threshold of sexual enlightenment. A young man's erotic education is enhanced by older women in "Wages of Sin," "A Dangerous Woman," and "Let Us Entertain You." The intricacies of life and love are explored by "A Lady I Met at Closing Time" and "In Good Hands." Vulnerability is revealed in "Hill Top Motel" and "Silent Heart." After reading "My Life as a Cowboy," you will understand that money can't buy love and that you should always hire a damn good lawyer.

I hope you will read on.

JeffreyStone

Age of Wisdom

My cousin Gloria was a pretty girl with dark hair and dark eyes. She was seventeen.

Sometimes, Gloria stayed the night at our house when my parents went out for the evening. My brother and my sister—who were eleven and nine—and I, nearly fourteen, were old enough not to need a sitter, but we all liked having Gloria with us because she was so much fun to be around. And Gloria liked to visit our house, where she got lots of attention from the guys in our neighborhood.

When Mother chided Gloria about *teasing those boys,* my cousin replied slowly and deliberately, rolling her eyes with all the innocence in the world, "Now Aunt Jeanie, you know I don't tease those boys—I wouldn't spit on them. 'Sides, I really think it's you they come to see, not me."

Mother would laugh at that and swat her niece on the buttocks with a dishtowel as they worked together in the kitchen, neither of them giving a thought to the two or three young men always sitting on the front porch waiting for Gloria to emerge, "like a pack of hounds after a bitch in heat," as Dad put it.

Most of the boys who came around to court Gloria were pretty good guys. At eighteen or nineteen, they were too old for her, I thought. But they kidded around with me—mostly to impress and curry favor with her, I suppose—so I didn't mind when they planted themselves, uninvited, in one of the wooden rocking chairs or in the swing on our front porch for the evening.

Usually, after the supper dishes were done, my mom, my dad, my siblings, and I sat on our front porch talking. Whenever Gloria visited, there were several suitors competing for an opportunity to spend the evening with Gloria, each doing his best to earn my father's blessings. I always stood next to her, and she put her arm around my shoulder. She told everyone that I was her sweetheart. We all laughed about that, because I was more than three years younger than Gloria and her third cousin to boot. But secretly, I wished that were not so and that I was a little older, because Cousin Gloria was as pretty a girl as you would find anywhere, and I liked being close to her.

On a typical fall evening, shortly after dark, my parents went into the house, leaving all of us youngsters on the front porch. Gradually, as night fell, everyone drifted away except for Gloria, me, and a couple of the older boys. Through some primordial instinct, one of the remaining boys opted himself out of competition for Gloria's favor and disappeared into the night. I too always sensed when it was time for me to leave Gloria with her chosen visitor alone. I excused myself demurely. She took her arm from around me, and moved to the swing beside the one she had selected by some process known only to her. Sometime later, when I looked through the screen door onto the porch, lighted faintly by only the street light more than half a block away, I saw their silhouettes close together on the swing. I couldn't help but wish that I was sitting next to her. The fact that she was my cousin was always in the back of my mind, but still I wanted to be near her, to smell her perfume and feel the soft warmth of her breasts against me when she hugged me.

One Saturday evening in the early fall, Gloria spent the night at our house while my parents were away for the weekend.

We had finished dinner just before twilight that evening, and I helped Gloria do the dishes. Afterward, we took our places on the front-porch swing as the sun melted out of sight. Several neighborhood boys and girls, including Clifford Hill, had migrated to our house, drawn by the knowledge that *no grownups were home*. Later in the evening, after the temperature had cooled, they drifted away one by one, until finally only Gloria, Clifford, and I were left in the swing. It wasn't long before all our talking stopped. After several minutes of silence, I realized I was no longer wanted. I quietly excused myself and went into the house and to bed.

I must have been asleep a half hour or more when I was awakened by Clifford's and Gloria's voices coming from the living room. At first, I tried to ignore them and go back to sleep, but I didn't succeed; I got out of bed and walked quietly to the doorway, where I could hear their conversation more clearly. I cracked open the door ever so slightly so I could see what was going on in the living room. Clifford was sitting on the sofa with Gloria on his lap. She had her arms around his neck and was kissing him on the lips. His left arm encircled her waist. He moved his other hand to her thigh while they continued to kiss.

I watched them for several minutes, my envy of Clifford deepening. I thought about my mother's assertion that, at thirteen, I had reached the age of wisdom, and she now expected some semblance of grown-up behavior out of me. But as far as I was concerned, I had just come into an age of ignorance, because I really didn't know anything about girls, no matter how much I wanted to. When I was around them, I experienced feelings I had never known before. Those feelings seemed to intensify when Cousin Gloria was around. And as I watched, I wished like anything that I was the one on the sofa with her. But it wasn't me; it was Clifford.

Gloria said suddenly, "Don't do that," as she pushed him away from her and quickly moved off his lap. As she sat next to him, pouting, I think she wanted him to believe she was angry with him, but I wasn't certain that she was angry at all.

Clifford reached for her, pulled her back on his lap, and kissed her again. I couldn't see what he did next, but I heard Gloria, sounding genuinely irritated, say, "I told you to stop that now."

I didn't hear either of them speak again for several minutes, and then I heard Gloria say, "You can't kiss me any more if you are going to do that."

Then, Clifford said confidently, "Who are you kidding? You like it, and you know it."

"No, I don't. I don't want you to do that!"

"Well, hell's bells," he said, raising his voice to a high falsetto, "you sure could've fooled me."

"You had better go home now," Gloria said. "It's getting late, and I have to go to bed."

I could tell from the tone of Gloria's voice that any ardor she might have had for Clifford prior to that moment had evaporated. I realized she really did want him to leave and that she was concerned the situation was getting out of hand. I continued to listen, hoping that he would leave the house without causing trouble.

Instead, I heard him say, "You mean you ain't goin' to do anything with me after all that stuff?"

"What stuff?"

"That stuff you've been letting me do."

"No, I'm not," she said, sounding desperate. "I couldn't do anything here in Aunt Jeanie's house even if I wanted to with all the kids at home."

"That didn't seem to stop you and Billy Taylor from doing it last week, right here in this house, did it now?"

Gloria said, "I don't know what you're talking about. I've never done anything with Billy Taylor here or any place else."

"Well, Billy said you did."

"He didn't say that; I know he didn't," Gloria protested.

"You know damn well he did too," Clifford said.

"If he did say it, he lied."

"Lied? My ass!"

"Well, I didn't do anything with him, but even if I did, I'm not doing it with you." Her voice was getting louder. "Now get out."

"You know what they call girls like you, don't you, Gloria?"

"No, I guess I don't."

"Prick teasers, that's what," Clifford said. "Prick teasers."

I dressed quickly and ran into the living room. Clifford had his back to me as he held Gloria down on the couch with his body on top of her. He attempted to kiss her, but she turned her face from side to side to prevent contact.

"Come on, prick teaser," he said. "This is one guy you ain't goin' to tease and get away with."

"Let her go," I yelled as I grabbed his shoulders, attempting to pull him away. He stood, towering above me, and struck the side of my head. Suddenly I was on the living room floor with Clifford standing over me.

"You little bastard," he said, as he hit me across the face with his open hand.

Shortly afterwards, I realized that Clifford had left the house. Gloria was wiping my bloody nose with a wet washcloth. My brother and sister were standing over me. My sister was crying.

It took a while for Gloria to settle all of us kids down. She made hot chocolate and turned on the radio. We sat together on the floor around the hearth, drinking our hot chocolate. Gloria put her arm around me and called me her hero. We all laughed and listened to the music on the radio in the dark living room, lighted by the flickering of the coal fire Gloria had made in the fireplace. Before too long, she said that it was time for all of us to go back to bed.

In the semidarkness, my brother and I talked for several minutes about my heroics, what I had done, and should have done, and so forth. Soon I heard him yawn and say something only half-intelligible. He didn't talk anymore; I knew he was asleep. I lay quietly for a bit longer before turning my face to the wall. Several minutes passed. Then Gloria came into our room and stood by my bed. I turned to look up at her. I could see her face in the light coming from the living room. She had been crying.

She sat on the edge of my bed, laid her hand gently on the side of my face, and said, "I'm so sorry, Jeff."

"You don't have to be sorry," I said, "You didn't do anything wrong."

"It was my fault you got hurt; thank you for coming to my rescue."

"You're welcome," I replied. I was completely lost for anything else to say, but my heart was bursting with pride and affection.

"Move over," she said, "and I will lie here with you until you go back to sleep."

I made room for her beside me and held back the cover as she climbed into bed. I turned my back to Gloria and sidled up against her. She put her arm around me. I lay there looking at the dark wall, oblivious to everything except the warmth of Gloria against me until I fell asleep.

I awoke a short time later to find Gloria sleeping beside me. I rose up on my elbow and looked at her face. I thought about her beauty and what a good person she was. My heart pounded in my chest as I watched her sleep, still fully clothed. I wanted to get very close to her, but I didn't dare wake her.

As hard as I tried, I couldn't understand what it was that Gloria wanted. No doubt she liked the attention she could get from all the different boys who came around our house, but it appeared to me that she didn't want to get serious with any of them. I had heard some of the braggadocio on our front porch, each boy trying to impress the other about how he had made out with Gloria. Yet I had seen for myself what happened when one of them tried to go too far with her. And even though I didn't want to, I could understand Clifford's frustration; as I had watched the two of them there in our living room, I had certainly believed that Gloria was going to allow him to do whatever he had the imagination to do. I was thoroughly puzzled. Still, as far as I was concerned, there wasn't anyone nicer or more considerate than Gloria.

As I lay on my elbow looking down on her sweet face, it took all the willpower I had to keep from kissing her and hugging her and telling her I wanted to make love to her, whatever that entailed, but I was afraid she would think I was a fool if I tried. I finally turned away from her and waited an eternity to go back to sleep.

I had slept for no more than an hour when I awoke again, this time to feel Gloria's legs warm against mine. I turned to face her and realized that she had removed her clothes except her panties and bra. Instantly, I was emboldened by the realization of what she was offering, and without any thought of rejection, I put my arm around her and pulled her body toward me. I felt her hand reach for me as she caressed me and moved closer. Instinctively, I pulled her panties aside and felt the soft, damp, mysterious warmth between her thighs. I moved on top of her, and as I lowered myself against her, she gently helped me inside. We held each other close as I kissed her neck and she breathed her moist breath into my hair.

When it was over, I held her for a while and then slowly moved away, turning my back to her once again. She put her arm around me while I lay quiet, basking in glorious bewilderment, unsure of what to say or whether I should say anything at all.

I understood how completely unselfish Gloria was; she had understood my feelings for her and had shown her gratitude the only way she knew how. In her way, she was showing me the pleasures that awaited me as I crossed over the threshold my mother called the age of wisdom. It was a moment I would relish forever, and Gloria would do nothing to diminish it for me. She would lie there, not speaking, letting me savor the feeling for as long as I wanted. Yet I knew that later she would probably have doubts about the wisdom of her act and perhaps about how discreet her young cousin might be. I thought I should say something to reassure her, speak just the right words to let her know her act of friendship and love was not wasted, that I had understood why it had happened. Finally, I said the only words that seemed appropriate: "That was my first time."

"I know," Gloria said.

"It was wonderful."

"I'm glad."

We were both silent again for several minutes.

Then I said in a whisper, "I won't ever tell anyone."

"I know," she said.

"Can we do it again sometime?"

"No," she said very quietly, holding me tightly," we mustn't."

The Conversion

I don't remember when I met Darla Ann Webster; I just came to know her when I was growing up. We were in the same grades together in school from the time we started the first grade, but it's funny that I can't remember ever being in a classroom with her. I do remember other things about Darla Ann though, and that's what this story is about.

When we were both about twelve years old, Darla Ann must have stood at least a head taller than me. She was a well-endowed girl with long legs and nicely formed breasts even then. From all indications, she reached puberty at least two years before I did, but by the time we both were approaching fifteen, I had finally caught up with her in every way but height.

Darla Ann had an older brother named William. Everyone in their family called him Willy, but I called him Goober like all the other guys who knew him. Even though Goober was two years older, we used to pal around together. He was an avid fox hunter, he and his dad. They kept a large, fenced dog pen, with a dozen or more doghouses and foxhounds, on the hillside above their house. Occasionally I would go with Goober and his dad to hunt fox at night. To this day, I don't know why they called it fox hunting, because on those outings I never saw anyone hunt anything. The men would sit around a huge fire and tell jokes, palaver, and drink moonshine. All the while, a pack of dogs would run through the hills barking, yapping, and howling. From time to time, someone would recognize a particular dog's howl.

"There goes Bathsheba," Goober's dad would say.

"Yep, and that sounds like Ole Blue with her," another hunter would add, spitting a stream of tobacco juice into the fire. "He's hot on the trail. They shore got a big 'un holed up this time."

Then they would listen by the fire and pick out the sounds of other dogs whose barks and howls they recognized and curse and spit some more. Goober and I lay in our sleeping bags, listening to the howling and the spitting and the profanity, just waiting for morning to come and perhaps a chance to pick up on a ribald joke that would be worth repeating to our buddies.

That was my experience with fox hunting, and I can't think of one thing I learned from it, except that you can get cold and stiff and sore from sleeping on the ground. But I did learn how dogs behave, especially female dogs. For example, when a female dog is amorous, male dogs for miles around can get wind of that fact and find their way to the female. It's kind of like that with women too. You take a woman who wants a man, and I guarantee you, even if she's stranded forty miles upriver, there'll be suitors from the four corners of the county, each trying to get his oar in the water first, so to speak.

That's how it was with Darla Ann I guess. When she was in the mood, it wasn't hard to tell. And on one of those occasions when the time was right, I happened to be the closest one to her and got there before anyone else did. I must have done something right, because afterward she would come looking for me or would find some excuse for us to be alone together when she was in one of those moods.

With a nod of her head or a toss of her hair, I would know what she had on her mind. We would go into the woods on the hill above her house, each taking separate paths, rendezvousing at a prearranged spot. Or we would slip away to the community garage at the end of our street or take advantage of her parents being gone or get together at my house when both my mother and my father were at work. It became routine for us to meet someplace for a fifteen- or twenty-minute session and then go our separate ways.

Darla Ann and I were never sweethearts; we didn't discuss love or getting married when we were grown or any such idealistic promises. Looking back, I suppose it was the least complicated relationship I ever had with a female. Everything was just fine between us until Darla got religion—and here's what led to that.

One Saturday afternoon, Darla Ann and I were sitting in her living room. She was all dressed up, having just returned from a shopping trip with her mother. I had not been in the room very long before I detected that feminine aura with which I had become so familiar, and I knew Darla Ann was ready for action. I moved across the room and stood next to her chair. After a moment or two, I pulled her dress up to her waist and slipped my hand into the top of her panties. Darla Ann must have thought we were taking a big chance of getting caught with her mother only two rooms away; she pulled my hand out of her panties and brushed down her dress with her hands.

"Let's go upstairs," she said.

"Are you crazy? Your mother is in the kitchen."

"It's OK. She won't think anything."

As we passed through the middle room and turned up the stairs, Darla Ann said, loud enough for her mother to hear, "We're going upstairs to find the Rook cards."

"Alright," her mother said, without finding out who, specifically, was going upstairs.

Darla proceeded me, and I climbed the stairs behind her. By the time I entered the door to her and her sister's bedroom, Darla Ann was standing in the middle of the room with her dress raised above her waist, showing off her long legs.

I made a beeline for her, unbuttoning my fly and standing on my tiptoes. But Darla Ann was still a couple of inches taller than me, and I couldn't get high enough by standing on my toes to reach her the way I wanted to.

"Let's get on the bed," I said.

"No, Mother will hear us."

"No, she won't; we'll be quiet."

Darla didn't want to waste time by lying on the bed, but she didn't want to waste an opportunity either, so she lay across the end of the bed with her feet nearly on the floor and her dress above her waist, holding her panties aside for me. At first, I was very quiet and moved gently against her without putting all my weight on top of her. But as conditions progressed and things became more heated, I soon forgot about being quiet or careful. As we were working ourselves toward the big finish, I brought my full weight down against Darla Ann and the bed.

With a loud crash, the bed slats fell to the floor. Darla Ann lay wedged among the mattress, springs, and slats canted at forty-five degrees in the air. I heard someone running up the stairs. By the time I buttoned my trousers and turned toward the door, Darla Ann's mother had reached the top of the stairs.

"Oh, my God," she said, holding her hands to her face, "What are you doing?" She almost cried seeing Darla still struggling to extricate herself from the broken bed.

"Nothing, Mrs. Webster; we were just sitting on the edge of the bed when it collapsed."

Mrs. Webster began wringing her hands. With a pained look on her face, she said to Darla, "We've got to talk about this," and then looking at me she said brusquely, "Go home!"

"Yes, ma'am," I said, backing out the doorway.

"And don't you tell anyone about this," she said. "I'll decide later what I'm going to do about it."

"Alright," I called to Mrs. Webster as I scurried down the stairs, "I won't."

In the living room, I stopped to listen to Darla Ann and her mother. "I don't know what I'm going to do with you, girl. I ought to tell your daddy, but I can't because he would beat you half to death if I did."

"I'm sorry, Mother," Darla Ann said. "We weren't doing what you think."

"I know better," Mrs. Webster said, "but I just don't know what to do about it."

"I'm sorry, Mother; I won't do it again."

"Not until you get another chance. I just don't know what to do with you, girl."

I could tell from the change in the loudness of her voice that she was walking toward the stairs. I quietly slipped across the room and out the door.

For the next several days, I didn't go near the Websters' house and didn't see Darla Ann. Every night at the supper table, I expected to hear my mother say, "Well, I talked with Darla Ann's mother today," but the words never arrived. After a while, I just assumed that Darla had convinced her mother nothing happened between us. No such luck—I found out the very next Sunday just what dire measures Mrs. Webster was taking to rehabilitate her wicked teenage daughter and rid her evermore of the temptation to copulate.

When I got to church that morning and took my place with my Sunday school class, I had been seated no more than five minutes when Mrs. Webster, Darla Ann, and her two younger sisters, Juniper and Blanch, arrived. I hadn't seen Mrs. Webster in church in forever. She didn't attend church very often because Mr. Webster didn't believe in it, and he didn't mince any words about his feelings. But I supposed that it was a case of drastic medicine for drastic ills; considering that Darla Ann's mother was risking the wrath of her fox- hunting (and sometimes coon-hunting) husband to change her daughter's ways, I understood just how serious a problem Mrs. Webster thought she had on her hands.

Sunday school was followed by church services. Pastor Dickerson announced that the text for his sermon, taken from the Psalms, was entitled "Stolen Water." It didn't take him long to get into the matter of fornication and how premarital sex can lead to all sorts of other sins, even murder, though God only knows how homicide can be tied in with hanky panky; just leave it up to a good fire- and-brimstone Baptist preacher to find a way to connect the two.

The pastor's sermon caught my undivided attention, and I had little doubt that either the Lord had told Pastor Dickerson everything or the pastor had been hiding under Darla Ann's bed just before it came crashing down. But I wasn't about to admit anything beyond what I had said to Mrs. Webster, and I hoped that Darla felt the same way. I sat on the edge of my seat, squirming, hoping the preacher would get to the end of his sermon without saying, "Jeff Stone, the Lord has revealed to me your evil ways; repent now before it's too late." I promised the Good Lord then and there that He and I would have a private conversation if He would just get Pastor Dickerson off the subject. I wasn't about to confess to everybody in the church. Darla Ann felt differently—she decided to get saved that Sunday morning and to confess every sin she had committed since the age of six.

When the choir finished the first verse of "Just As I Am" and launched into the chorus, Darla Ann got happy. She began to shout, pushing past the people standing in her pew and hurrying toward the altar; her mother, hanging onto Darla's long white dress, followed close behind. As they knelt together at the altar, several of the church sisters knelt, flocked around them, eager to assist Darla to throw off the horrific bonds of sin. Pastor Dickerson knelt next to her, speaking of angels rejoicing at the return of one lost sheep to the fold. Then he asked her to confess her sins, her many sins, which she seemed inclined to do at the urging of her mother and the church sisters.

I hoped selfishly that the conversion of Darla Ann was not too thorough and that she did not intend to completely mend all her ways. When the pastor asked for her confession, I assumed it would be stated only in generalities. But if I had thought more about it, I would have known she couldn't get away with that. When it comes to forgiving sins, the Baptists won't settle for generalities; they want specifics.

Darla commenced a grinding chronology of a sinful life starting the day after she began the first grade, including in detail how she had started having sex at the age of twelve and how it had gotten out of control because the devil got control of her. The preacher assured her that she was not completely at fault, that it takes two to tango, and that he knew she was a good God-fearing girl who must have been led astray by some older, evil boys; of course the pastor wanted their names.

As she rattled off a list of a dozen or so names, I cringed, sitting there next to my mother just waiting to hear "Jeffrey Stone" come rolling off Darla's tongue. I knew my mother would have been embarrassed to death if her son had been included in that list of fornicators; then, after church, I would have had my ear torn from the side of my head and would have been scheduled for a belt whipping by my dad. I was prepared to run for the altar and ask the preacher for absolution as soon as I heard the first syllable of my name. That, or to run for the door and head for Texas at a fast trot. But thanks be to the patron saint of teenage dabblers, Darla never mentioned my name.

Darla's confessions had an exhilarating effect on the rest of the congregation; soon the altar was engulfed with resurrected saints and new converts, all clamoring to be heard testifying and admitting to all manner of wrongs, most of them minor in comparison to the eyebrow-raising sins told by Darla only minutes before. It was probably an opportune time to unburden oneself in detail, knowing full well that the confession would be little remembered in light of Darla's startling revelations.

Just before the services ended, the pastor announced a baptism set for the following Sunday at the dam in the creek nearby the church. He then formed a receiving line with Darla on one side of him and her mother on the other, accompanied by members who had rededicated themselves. The rest of the congregation paraded by, shaking the preacher's hand and hugging the converts. I got in line behind my mother, and we worked our way up to Darla Ann. When I reached the spot in front of her, I hugged her good and then shook the preacher's hand. As soon as I was in front of Mrs. Webster, a terrible coughing spell came over me, bending me over double for several seconds. By the time I had finished coughing, mother had led me on through the receiving line and out the door of the church.

The next Sunday, after church services, the congregation walked from the church to the baptismal dam singing "Amazing Grace." All the new converts—two young boys, an elderly gentleman, Darla, and three other girls—were dressed in white. Darla Ann was the tallest girl to be baptized. She looked truly saintly, standing there barefoot with a new glow to her as the preacher held out his hand to lead her into the water; as she stood waist deep with the preacher's left arm around her, his right hand raised in the air, I must say that I felt the sanctity of the moment; when he lowered his right arm and placed his hand over her nose and mouth to submerge her under the water, I felt a surge of remorse and guilt that lasted until Darla Ann came out of the water with her wet clothes sticking to her body, clearly revealing the outline of her breasts and the line of her bikini panties against her rotund derriere. I was relieved to see her mother place a large towel around her, thereby putting an end to the possibility of any sacrilegious distractions.

After that Sunday, Darla Ann and her sisters became regular churchgoers. They attended Sunday school and morning church services every week. Darla Ann was active in all sorts of church activities; she sang in the choir, worked on charity drives, and visited the shut-ins. Before long, it was the accepted wisdom that the Lord had performed a conversion almost as astonishing as that of St. Paul. He had taken a budding harlot to his bosom and had transformed her into a quasi saint. She was loved by all the members of the church and greatly admired for her grand transformation; after all, if it could happen to such a sinner as Darla Ann, it could happen to anyone.

I really didn't know what to think about it, so I tried not to. After knowing Darla in such a personal way, it took a little doing for me to envision her as a saint of the church.

Nevertheless, if she truly had changed as much as was thought by everyone, I was happy for her. And so, I gradually fell in line with the rest of the congregation and almost forgot about all the things that had happened between us.

I can recall how Darla's name came to be spoken with near reverence. In church, we whispered in her presence. The older ladies called her "darling" and "dear" and tiptoed around her. I believe if she had been Catholic, the Blessed Virgin would have appeared side by side with her; and quite possibly it may have been difficult to tell them apart, except that Darla Ann probably would have been the taller one.

Before long, Mrs. Webster had welcomed me back as a visitor to her home, and I no longer felt uneasy in her presence. She apparently was satisfied that Darla Ann's past was truly past and that no amount of temptation would cause her to go astray again. That was good enough for me.

* * *

Kick-the-Can was a game the kids on our street played almost every summer evening at dusk. The can, usually a Pet Milk tin, was placed under the streetlight in front of the Websters' house. When the can was kicked, we would all run for our favorite hiding places. The more serious players, especially the boys who lifted weights and took pride in their athletic prowess, would hide in spots that enabled them to run quickly to the can, and with form and grace worthy of a professional field goal kicker, send it tumbling down the blacktop for one hundred feet or more. The lovers among us would hide in the bushes or under a house and hold hands and kiss and mess around until someone found us and made one of us "It". That's what Darla Ann and I used to do, but no more.

This time when we played Kick-the-Can, Darla Ann ran to hide all alone, and of course I had nothing to do but to play the game seriously, which I did for as long as I could stand it. After about the third or fourth time I kicked the can, I ran to hide in the tall shrubbery along Darla Ann's fence, right next to her front porch where her visiting grandmother sat in her rocking chair. As I crawled along the fence in the deepening twilight, I ran into Darla Ann on her hands and knees in the flower bed just ahead of me. I was almost upon her, my nose ready to collide with her rear end, before I realized who it was. We began to whisper about being quiet, how much fun the game was, and how hard I had kicked the can last time.

As we made small talk and touched ever so incidentally, I was almost certain I detected a whiff of the old Darla, but I was more than reluctant to broach the subject, having been witness to the recent miracle at our church. For several minutes we sat in the flower bed, leaning back against the fence talking quietly. When Darla again got on her hands and knees to crawl in the direction of the street, I proceeded behind her, occasionally bumping against her backside with my face, careful not to be too bold.

"I wish you wouldn't do that," she whispered, looking back over her shoulder at me.

"Sorry. I didn't mean to."

As we got closer to the street near the front porch, both of us poised to run and kick the can, I realized there probably would not be another opportunity like the present one, and so, throwing caution to the wind, I said, "Can I ask you something?"

"Yes; what?"

"Do you still like to fuck?"

"Grandma will hear you," she said, pointing to the wrinkled old woman slowly rocking back and forth in the shadows of the front porch above us.

"Well, do you?"

Darla got up from the flower bed and ran toward the Pet Milk can, kicking it into the next county. As the girl who was "It" ran to get the can, Darla dashed around the opposite side of her house, apparently to find a new hiding place as far away from me as she could get.

Even though I was concealed by the bushes, I felt like a naked infidel, exposed to a leering world. I sat for a few moments reflecting on my terrible behavior, especially toward someone who obviously had changed so dramatically. I thought surely I would be struck by lightening or have my tongue swell to four times its normal size or, worse yet, be made impotent at an early age. I could have kicked myself for being so stupid. But at least I knew that as kind and good as Darla Ann had become in her converted state, she would forgive me and probably would not tell anyone what I had dared ask her.

I made up my mind then and there that I would apologize to her and beg her forgiveness as soon as I had a chance. For now, I was through with Kick-the-Can; the game was over, and I was ready to get straight up out of the shrubbery and walk home.

Just then I heard the rustling of bushes only a few feet from me and looked to see Darla Ann crawling toward me on her hands and knees.

Silent Heart

O dell Reese was twenty-three, long legged, and handsome, with dark hair that grew just down over the tops of his ears and onto his collar. He wore a permanent smile. When he met you for the first time, he shook your hand as if he was trying to crush it and at the same time pull your arm right off your shoulder. It didn't take him long to make friends. Shortly after moving to town, he knew everybody on our street and was liked by everyone. However, there was a dark side to Odell not revealed by his charming bucolic ways.

Odell didn't hold a steady job, but he never seemed to lack for money. If he had an identifiable occupation, it would have been that of a truck driver. When he wasn't away on an overnight or weekend trip in his pickup truck, he could be found on a baseball field or in his backyard playing basketball. His friends, a conglomeration of misfits, were all several years younger than he.

"He just never grew up," most people said, or they decided that he was making up for the youth he lost while serving in Vietnam. Whatever their cause, his activities deprived his wife, Linda, and baby son, six-month-old Michael, of any significant portion of his attention or concern.

Odell's excursions ostensibly took him to a town about sixty miles away, but no one really knew his true destination. He was usually accompanied by one or two members of his gang.

They would return with tales of conquest and debauchery, having allegedly stayed the night or weekend with "some gorgeous women" in a motel. These reports elevated Odell in the eyes of his gang and inspired envy in those who had not been privileged to participate.

Everyone, particularly the residents on our street, conjectured about Odell's true vocation. As always happens in small towns, the time he spent away from home set tongues wagging and people guessing about what he actually did for a living. Some folks opined that he was hauling moonshine whiskey; others thought something much more insidious, such as marijuana or cocaine; still others suggested he was working for the CIA. But for all their voiced suspicions, their admiration and fondness for Odell did not appear to wane.

When I first met him, I, like most other people, succumbed to his apparent good nature. However, after I got to know him better, witnessed his abusive treatment of Linda, and observed his neglect of Michael, I no longer admired him.

Linda was a deaf-mute, unable to speak except for hollow sounds that emanated from the back of her mouth when she became excited. Neither she nor anyone around her ever learned sign language. She communicated by reading lips and responding with handwritten notes. At seventeen, she met and married Odell; a year later, Michael was born.

I was one of the teenagers who played basketball with Odell in his backyard, but I was never a part of his inner circle. It was during our pickup ball games that I witnessed his disrespect toward and mistreatment of his wife. That was when I decided he was not someone I wanted to emulate.

"Hey, dummy," he said loudly one hot afternoon during one of our games, "get me and the boys something to drink."

Linda was sitting on the back steps, holding Michael on her lap. She apparently had not been watching Odell and had not read his lips. She gestured with one hand in front of her, indicating that she did not understand. Odell became irate and threw the ball in her direction. It bounced off the bottom step and rolled across the yard.

She got up with the baby in her arms and walked defiantly into the house.

"Dumb cunt!" Odell screamed as he pursued the ball, his insult eliciting laughter from the other players.

I wanted to say something in defense of Linda, but I didn't. Odell stood head and shoulders above me and could easily have given me a beating if I dared to interfere. I decided that the least I could do was show my disapproval by quitting the game. I never played basketball with Odell and his gang again.

Afterward, Linda became my obsession. I thought of her constantly and worried that Odell would do something to harm her and the baby. I couldn't understand why anyone as beautiful and sweet as Linda ever married Odell. I reasoned that he possessed powers of persuasion with women that I couldn't comprehend. Ultimately, I concluded that she must have considered herself damaged goods because of her deafness and had settled for the first man who asked her to marry him.

In Linda, Odell found someone whom he could dominate almost completely. She had no friends of her own, since nearly everyone who came to her house was one of Odell's gang. She could not understand what was being said in her presence unless it was spoken directly to her. He could dress her up like a porcelain doll and show her off without any concern that someone else might want her; after all, who would find a deaf-mute desirable, no matter how beautiful she was? Perhaps I was the only one, but I thought she was the prettiest girl I had ever seen. I was very much in love with her, but I was only sixteen.

When Odell was away, I invented reasons to visit Linda. I helped her with chores and made trips to the grocery store, which was more than a mile away. She was always happy to have someone who would keep her company. As our friendship deepened, I learned that she still had hopes and dreams like those of all young girls. This discovery gave me even more cause to wonder why she had ever married Odell, and I was happily convinced that she didn't love him.

We communicated by exchanging notes. She kept a small writing pad with her at all times. We would scribble notes and riddles and draw stick people or silly cartoons. Sometimes when she was really pleased with something I did or said, she would mouth words to me and put both her hands on the sides of my face to make me laugh out loud while she made noises that sounded like echoes.

One Saturday evening late in the fall, we were exchanging notes and making up riddles. Michael was in bed, and Linda and I were sitting on the back porch steps with just enough light coming through the open kitchen door to let us see our notes. We were positioned close enough to benefit from each other's body heat as the sun went down over the hill behind the house. I handed her a riddle, scribbled haphazardly across a note pad.

> *One night while walking in the rain,*
> *I met a man who came from Spain;*
> *He tipped his hat and drew his cane;*
> *In this riddle, I have said his name.*

What is it?

She took the note from me and, putting her finger on each word, went over and over each line. Finally, hiding the pad on her opposite side, she scribbled a word and then held the pad up for me to see in the dim light. She had written "Cain."

I said, "No, try again."

Quickly, she scribbled, "Cain, the Bible, Cain and Abel."

I turned my face to her, smiling. "No," I said slowly, "there's another answer; try again."

She wrote down her new answer and handed it to me. "Riddle, like Tex Riddle?"

I laughed and wrote on the pad. "His name is Tex R-I-T-T-E-R, not R-I-D-D-L-E.

She began to laugh with me, turning her head away so that I couldn't see her embarrassment. Again, she put her finger on each word as she carefully read the lines over and over. After a few minutes, she smiled at me and said aloud, in words almost perfectly formed, "I give up."

I was delighted that she hadn't guessed my riddle and thrilled that she had actually attempted to speak to me. "Andrew," I said, "and drew his cane." I showed her the riddle and ran my finger under the words *and drew*.

She began to laugh again, making sounds that she would have thought embarrassing in the company of most people.

Seeing her laugh was exhilarating and made me realize just how much I enjoyed being with her. Her response to the simple things we were doing made me see her as someone my own age. I had the urge to put my arms around her and kiss her, but I didn't want her to know that such thoughts were moving through my mind.

She laughed again and slapped me on the arm in mock anger; then pointing her finger at her chest, she mouthed, "My turn," and began to scribble on the pad. When she finished, she handed it to me and, with laughter, hid her face in her hands. I looked at the verse she had written:

> *There was a monkey sitting on a bench*
> *Screwing his dick with a monkey wrench*

I recognized it as part of a ditty that I thought only boys knew. "Finish it," I said, handing the note back to her.

"No! It's too dirty," she said, peeking at me through her fingers.

We both laughed until there was nothing more to laugh about; then we fell into an interminable silence. We sat with our shoulders close together, our heads touching, each not daring to look at the other. I couldn't begin to guess what she was thinking, but I was lost in a euphoria I had never felt before. Finally, we somehow found the courage to look deeply and honestly at each other, acknowledging that something special was happening between us. I took her hand in mine and held it awkwardly.

After several minutes, she removed her hand from mine and wrote on the notepad. She kept the note hidden from me until she had gotten up from the steps. At the kitchen door, she handed me the paper. I arose and moved into the light where I read what she had written: "I hope Odell never comes back."

She could read my lips when I replied, "Don't say that; you don't mean it."

"Yes, I do," she mouthed, nodding her head with the innocence of a small child.

Then she suddenly appeared scared, I guess afraid I might tell someone what she had just said. She placed her hands on my upper arms as if to control me, and, shaking her head from side to side, said without making a sound, "Don't tell Odell; please don't tell Odell."

"I never would," I said slowly.

"Or your mother," she said, motioning a warning with her finger.

"I wouldn't."

She quickly scribbled another note, folded it, and handed it to me, then walked out of the kitchen into the bedroom. I unfolded the note and read it. "Have you ever made love to a girl?"

I followed her into the bedroom, where she stood with her back to me. I put my hands on her shoulders and turned her to face me. "Once," I said, holding the notepad, "only once." I held one finger up to make certain she understood.

She quickly put her arms around my neck, and I held her against me, my arms encircling her waist. We embraced that way for several minutes, she, I suppose, wondering about the wisdom of her actions and I simply not knowing what she wanted me to do next. She took the pad from my hand, scribbled another note, and handed it to me: "Would you like to make love to me?"

"Yes, if you want me to."

We sat on the edge of the bed, a few feet from the crib where Michael slept. She walked to the crib, looked down at him, and adjusted the covers around him. I watched her intently as she turned off the light, leaving the bedroom in near darkness, dimly illuminated only by the light coming from the kitchen. She kneeled on the floor in front of me and began to unbutton my trousers. She caressed me with her hands through my underwear and breathed her warm breath against my open trousers. I ran my fingers through her hair in anticipation of something wonderful that I had never experienced. Suddenly, she stopped and slowly rebuttoned my pants. She began to sob and shake uncontrollably, her head lying limp against my legs.

"It's alright," I said, as I helped her to her feet.

She took the pad from the nightstand and scribbled a note. While I read it in the dim light that shone through the doorway, she wiped tears from her eyes.

"I'm sorry," it read.

"Please don't be." I placed my hands on her shoulders, and looked into her face. "I understand."

I became aware of someone knocking at the door. At first it seemed far away. I listened and realized it was coming from the front of the house. Although Linda couldn't have heard it, she sensed that someone was at the door.

"The door," she said, falling to her knees.

"What are you doing?" I asked, tilting her chin so she could see me as I spoke.

"Praying," she mouthed.

"Why?"

"'Cause I am a bad wife."

The knocking persisted, getting louder as it continued.

I ran to open the door. There were two policemen standing on the porch; one held a flashlight, which he shined at my feet. I recognized him as the county sheriff.

"What's the problem, Sheriff?"

"We're looking for Mrs. Reese; is she home?"

"She's home, but she won't be able to understand you—She's deaf."

"We need to talk with her."

"You'll have to talk to me; Mrs. Reese won't understand what you're saying."

"Who are you?"

"I'm Jim Gardner; I help Mrs. Reese while her husband is away working."

"Your dad George Gardner?"

"Yes, sir."

"We have to let Mrs. Reese know there's been an accident."

"What kind of accident?"

"Wreck … involving her husband. Isn't Odell her husband?

"Yes."

"He and two other boys were killed. Couple of other people hurt bad."

I stood emotionless for a moment, stunned, but somehow not surprised that Odell would come to such an end.

The sheriff put his hand on my shoulder and patted me comfortingly. "Mrs. Reese will have to come down to the hospital tomorrow morning to identify him and make arrangements with the funeral home."

"She has no way to get there," I said, coming to the realization that Linda and Michael would now be all alone.

"We'll pick her up at nine o'clock," the sheriff said, "You sure you don't want us to break the news to her?"

"No, I'd better tell her."

"OK. Let her know how sorry we are; I'll pick her up at nine … You sure you don't want us to stay for a while?"

"No."

The sheriff and his deputy walked down the steps to their car.

I returned to the bedroom and looked in. Linda was still kneeling on the floor with her eyes closed and her hands folded against the bed. When I heard the sheriff's car drive past the house and head back into town, I sat down at the kitchen table and began to write on the pages of the notepad.

I thought about all the things we had discussed earlier that evening, about Odell not coming home and all. I wondered if God really did intervene in people's lives or if everything that happens to us happens by chance. I was certain that Linda would believe she had brought about Odell's death just by wishing he would never come back home. And even though she really didn't mean what she had said, she probably would blame herself for the rest of her life. I wrote a note to Linda describing the accident, adding words I hoped would comfort her. I told her she should not blame herself, that no one on earth could control such events. Because of all his traveling and drinking, it had become just a matter of time before Odell suffered a serious accident. I tried to express my own sadness, but as much as I wanted to, I could not feel a sense of loss in his death, only concern about what would become of his wife and his son.

When I finished writing, I went to the bedroom and seated myself next to Linda on the bed.

"Who was at the door?" she asked, looking up at me from her kneeling position. I could tell from the anguish in her face that she knew everything even before I handed her the note.

"God," I said, extending the piece of paper toward her.

Linda got off the bed as she read my note. The expression on her face never changed. Halfway through the message, tears began to run down her face, but she never made a sound. When she finished reading, she pressed the note to her heart and wiped the tears away with her open hand. Then she reached for a pencil on the night stand and wrote something, which she held up for me to read.

"I knew it was God," the note said. She mouthed the words: "I knew."

She took my hand and led me to the crib in the corner of the room. We stood, holding hands, looking down at Michael sleeping peacefully. Linda cried quietly for several minutes before she wiped her eyes. Then, smiling sadly, she began slowly to remove her dress.

"Turn out the light," she said.

Hitchhiker

The Friday-night movie in Jenkins had lasted longer than I expected. My friends had gone off drinking, and I was left to get home the best way I could. It was nearly eleven o'clock, much too late for a sixteen-year-old boy to be alone alongside a country road. I stuck my thumb out, begging a ride with the first person going my way.

The black Ford pickup stopped in front of me with its right tires off the paved highway. The driver leaned across the seat and opened the door. I stepped quickly to the truck, took hold of the door handle, and with one foot on the running board, hoisted myself onto the seat next to Jarvis Moon. I had second thoughts once I realized who he was, but it was too late to decline the ride.

"Uh, goin' to Caraway?" I asked cautiously, knowing that he lived there, not more than a half mile from my house.

"Yeah," he said, "I am. You live there?"

"Yeah, Mr. Moon. Joey Randolph—I deliver the newspaper to your dad. Didn't you recognize me before you stopped?"

"Sure, sure. I just didn't remember your name." I knew he was lying.

He glanced at me and smiled through menacing, week-old stubble.

I had never met Jarvis Moon before that night, but I had seen him, and I had heard about him. He had a reputation for liking the company of young boys, and he often drove around town with several teenage boys in the front seat and in the back of his truck. I don't know whether Jarvis ever did anything wrong with those boys, but that didn't matter, because to almost everyone in our community, it just didn't look right.

I delivered the *Knoxville News Sentinel* in our town. Jarvis's parents were my customers. Although I threw a paper on their front porch every day and stopped to collect once a week, I had never seen thirty-something- year-old Jarvis at their house. I had only seen him from a distance as he drove by in his truck. But there I was, sitting on the front seat on a pitch-black road between Jenkins and Caraway, wondering what I would do if he attempted to accost me.

We drove in silence for about two miles, I suppose, because we didn't have much in common to talk about. I was probably too intimidated by Jarvis to say anything, and I could only imagine that he was busy thinking of ways to dispose of my body.

He broke the silence with, "Hungry?"

Before I could answer, he drove past the turnoff to Caraway.

"Where we headed?" I asked, looking at him while trying to control my unwieldy imagination.

He looked straight ahead as he responded. "Neonna. Carl's Diner. They make good burgers ... You could use one, couldn't you?"

"Sure," I said, "but I need to get home; my mother will be worried."

"Won't take long."

Fifteen minutes later, we were seated in a booth in Carl's Diner. We ate our hamburgers in silence and washed them down with Coke. Jarvis paid the waitress, who doubled as a cashier. He picked up two Hershey candy bars from a box by the register and handed the waitress the dollar he had just received in change. "Keep the change," he said.

We made our way back to the truck, and Jarvis struck out, driving in the direction of Caraway while we ate our Hershey bars. Five minutes after turning up Caraway Fork, he pulled off the side of the road, opened the door, and stepped down out of the truck.

"I gotta take a leak," he said, looking back through the open door at me. "How about you?"

"Me too," I said. I got out of the truck on the passenger side.

I didn't notice Jarvis walking around the truck to where I stood. But I suddenly felt his ominous presence behind me.

He put his hands on my shoulders and spoke calmly. "Don't worry; I won't hurt you."

Instinctively, I broke from his grasp, turned, and ran back to the graveled road. I thought if I could just make it to the railroad tracks, I could find a place to hide between the gondolas. But then I thought of my mother and how she would never again be able to sleep if something bad happened to me. I knew I had to get home where she would still be waiting up. So I started running up the road toward home. The sliver of a moon that had been visible only moments before was suddenly hidden behind heavy rain clouds, making it almost impossible to see the road.

After a few moments, headlights shone from behind my back and on the road ahead of me as Jarvis's truck quickly gained ground. I watched my shadow enlarge and elongate, then disappear as the truck passed me and pulled off the road just up ahead. I saw the dark figure of Jarvis get down out of the truck and walk toward me. He had a flashlight in his hand.

Suddenly rain began to fall in torrents; lightning flashed across the railroad yard, lighting up the dark gondolas filled to overflowing with coal. I wondered if "C & O Rail Road" might be the last words I would ever read. I slid into the drainage ditch running between the graveled road and the main railroad track and squatted down. I waited for Jarvis to find me and do whatever he had planned.

"Come on, Joey," he said, stretching out his arm, offering me his open hand. "I'll take you home." There was a plea in his voice that told me I had nothing to fear.

I climbed up the embankment and followed him back to the truck. The engine was still running. Jarvis turned on the windshield wipers and put the transmission into gear. We drove in silence for a few minutes, then he spoke. "I didn't mean anything."

I didn't reply.

"I didn't mean to scare you. I really didn't mean anything … You've got to believe me." He drove into the rain without taking his eyes off the road.

"It's OK," I said dispassionately.

"You've got to promise not to tell anyone, 'cause I didn't mean anything by it ... OK?"

"OK," I said again, "I won't tell anyone."

"Not even your mother."

"OK."

"Promise?"

"Yeah, I promise."

* * *

I never told anyone about my encounter with Jarvis Moon, not even my brother, who was two years older than I, and in whom I confided everything. I didn't want anyone to know I was parked alone with Jarvis beside the road at midnight.

Three weeks after the incident, I saw him when I was delivering the evening paper. As I rode by on my bicycle, I threw the rolled-up newspaper toward the porch, just as I always did. This time, I missed my mark and knocked a pot of ferns off the wooden railing. The pot broke with a thud, showering the porch with black dirt and evergreen ferns. I immediately stopped and laid the bicycle on its side. As I approached the gate, Jarvis emerged from behind the screen door.

"You little bastard," he yelled. "What do you think you're doing?"

I was ready to apologize, to offer to pay for the damage, but I couldn't find the words to say that I was sorry. The only thoughts I had were of the terror, real or imagined, Jarvis had inflicted on me a few weeks earlier.

"Fuck you, you goddamn queer," I said, as I lifted my bicycle out of the dirt. I got on and rode away.

Over the years, I have thought about Jarvis Moon, about how lonely he must have been, living amidst the prejudice and bigotry of our small town. I have wondered if my fears that night were justified or if my homophobia created a monster that existed only in my mind. And I have imagined that many objects and names were hurled at his door. Perhaps the broken pot of ferns was just the final straw. I will never know.

Less than a month later, Jarvis Moon, his father, and his mother moved from our town.

The Principle of the Thing

E mma Lou and I became good friends the spring we finished our sophomore year of high school. That was when I began mowing the lawn for her mother every weekend. As part of my compensation, I was allowed to ogle Emma, her sisters, and her mother as they sunbathed in the backyard and I mowed around them. The breaks I took from mowing gave me an opportunity to learn some of their innermost secrets while we drank iced tea and discussed small-town gossip.

Mrs. Puckett was an attractive woman just past forty, though her age was not evident in her appearance. Her manner of dress always accentuated her good looks, revealed her buxom shape, and made her enticingly sensual to me. All three of the girls had figures much like their mother's, and they dressed similarly. Anyone seeing them together for the first time would have found it difficult to distinguish the mother from her three very appealing daughters.

Eve Puckett had high hopes for her three girls, Imogene, Thelma, and the youngest, seventeen-year-old Emma Lou. She wanted all of them to marry well. Accordingly, she discouraged them from dating local boys, most of whom were destined to spend their lives working in the canning factory the way their fathers did.

"No daughter of mine is going to marry a factory worker," she often said. "I want you to better yourselves and not spend your lives in this godforsaken town."

And who could blame her? I didn't. The girls had beauty, personality and practiced poise. It was hard to fault Mrs. Puckett for encouraging her daughters to use their physical assets, charm, and grace to attract matrimonial candidates from families who lived on Lakeside, where the doctors, attorneys, and other more prosperous professionals of our town resided. My future financial prospects dimmed any hope I might have had for a romantic relationship with one of the girls, who, I suppose, viewed me as the younger brother they never had. Nevertheless, their viewpoint did not prevent me from wildly fantasizing as I watched them rubbing suntan oil on each other while I mowed the lawn.

Although Mrs. Puckett encouraged her girls to be seductive, she continually cautioned them against promiscuity.

"Don't let yourselves be taken for granted," she was fond of saying. "The longer you hold out, the more apt you are to get a man to marry you."

That seemed to be sound advice for all the girls except Emma Lou, who quickly gained a reputation for dropping her drawers for everyone she dated, and usually on the first date. When Mrs. Puckett heard the rumors about her daughter, she reacted by putting a halt to Emma's dating: "No more dates by yourself until you are eighteen."

Of course, this dictum had a most deleterious effect on Emma Lou's newly acquired appetite for sex, and it seriously impaired her popularity. But Eve Puckett stood her ground and allowed Emma Lou to go on dates only when chaperoned by one of her older sisters.

* * *

One Saturday, I finished mowing the lawn late in the afternoon and just happened to linger at the Puckett house talking with the girls until sunset. I was about to get on my bicycle and ride off when Mrs. Puckett called me aside and asked me for a favor.

"Imogene and Thelma have dates tonight, and I won't be coming home until after midnight," she said. "Can you keep Emma Lou company until one of the girls gets home?"

Perhaps I had so successfully disguised my lechery when exposed to the Puckett's backyard pulchritudinous feasts that Eve believed I was a eunuch or gay; she obviously thought I was incapable of violating her youngest daughter's reestablished virginal ways. And I, of course, acquiesced to ensure that Emma Lou would remain abstinent for at least one whole evening. Emma expressed her disappointment by protesting that the arranged night at home would render her an old maid before her time, which did not speak highly of my sexual appeal to her.

When we were alone in the house, we busied ourselves with mundane activities that had little chance of initiating or enhancing romantic notions. We listened to rock and roll, worked crossword puzzles, and looked through family albums; we finally made sandwiches for supper.

When we had finished eating, Emma came up with a suggestion out of the blue. "Let's dance," she said.

"OK," I said, thinking, "Why not?"

Without blinking an eye, she walked over to the record player, began looking through a stack of LPs, and asked, "What do you want to hear?"

"Anything slow," I said. "I'm not a good dancer."

She put a stack of records on, walked to the couch where I was sitting, and reached her arms toward me, inviting me to dance. I put my arm on her waist and she rested her head on my shoulder. We began to gently move around the living room. I heard the pleasant sound of her occasional hum to the music. Now and then she'd squeeze my hand and press herself against me. Her breasts were warm and pliant against my shirt. Her soft brown hair smelled like flowers. Before long, it was obvious that I was being affected by her proximity.

"We'd better stop," I said.

"No, I like it," Emma Lou said, snuggling closer.

We danced a few more steps, then stopped and kissed.

"We shouldn't have done that," I said, taking her by the hand and starting to move around the floor again.

We had danced only a few minutes longer before she stopped moving and put both arms around my neck. We stood in the middle of the room, embracing and kissing passionately.

"We had better stop," I said, stepping back from her but not letting go of her hand. I didn't mean what I was saying, because there was a part of me that refused to allow me to move too far away.

As we stood at arm's length, I looked at her. She was as desirable as a girl could ever be—rosy cheeks, voluptuous smile, sparkling eyes—and we were alone in the house.

"Come on," she said, holding my hand and walking toward the stairs, "let's go upstairs."

"I don't think we should," I said, resigned to the probability that we would. "What would your mother think if she knew what we were doing?"

"Mother won't know."

"I will, though; she trusted me to stay with you and keep you out of trouble," I said, hoping Emma Lou would convince me that my only obligation was to keep her company and that I had no responsibility to save her from her own moral failures.

"It's ok," she said. "This is my decision, not Mother's."

"Don't you think your mother wants what's best for you?"

"I know what's best for me," she said. "Besides, my mother thinks the world of you. She would love for you and me to be sweethearts."

"I don't think so," I said. "I won't ever have money."

"But she still likes you a lot. Don't you know that?"

"Yes, but she doesn't want you to marry me; that's for sure."

Emma Lou moved back into my arms and kissed me again. Then, giggling, she pulled my head down toward her face and breathed her warm breath into my ear. She held my hand as she slowly led me upstairs to her bedroom. I followed a half step behind.

We lay across her bed holding each other close, caressing and kissing. I heard her say, "I love you, Jeff."

I almost responded, "I love you too, Emma Lou," but I contemplated what I was about to say before I spoke the words.

She appeared to wait for me to reply. When I didn't, she asked, "Did you hear what I said? I said 'I love you.'"

I kissed her, hoping that my passion would communicate my feelings sufficiently to save me from telling a lie. I put my hand under her skirt. When I moved my fingers tenderly up the inside of her thigh, she pushed my hand away.

"Are you in love with me, Jeff Stone?" she asked, looking up at me, half-smiling, subtly demanding an answer.

"Emma Lou, you know how much I like you," I said. "You are one of my best friends, and I love you as a friend."

"I didn't ask you if you love me; I asked you if you're in love with me; there's a big difference."

"Well I can't say if I am or if I'm not," I equivocated, sensing that the opportunity I had wished for all summer was about to slip away.

"Do you love me or don't you, Jeff?"

She seemed so desperate to have someone tell her he loved her, but I just couldn't bring myself to do it. As much as I wanted to have sex with her, I couldn't lie to her.

"Emma Lou, I can't tell you I'm in love with you."

"Why not?"

"Because I'm not."

The very last thing I wished to do was to hurt her feelings. It would have been easy to tell her I was in love with her. She was beautiful, desirable, and willing. I could have said it; I had done worse things. It would have been like meeting a girl somewhere on vacation, someone you would know for only a few days or a week, and saying the things you needed to say to entice her to fool around with you, then sending her home to her boyfriend when vacation was over. I couldn't do that to Emma Lou; I would have to face her and her mother almost every day, perhaps for the rest of my life. I was not in love with her, and I cared too much for her to tell her a lie.

"I love you, Emma Lou, but I'm not in love with you. Do you understand?"

"Don't you want to make love to me?" she asked, as she began to remove her blouse.

"Yes," I said nodding my head, looking at her breasts above the lace of her bra. "I would be a fool if I didn't want to, wouldn't I?"

"Well, I do have some pride, you know, and I won't make love with anyone who isn't in love with me, and that's that."

"I don't think you would want me to tell you I'm in love with you if I don't mean it," I reasoned with her, unable to tear my eyes away as she raised her back off the bed and removed her skirt. She turned onto her stomach and rested her head on a pillow. Then she reached one hand behind her back and unfastened her bra. It was, obviously, something she had done before.

I was already taking off my trousers by the time she turned to look at me, holding her bra up for me to see. I quickly lay on the bed beside her and began kissing her breasts.

"Are you in love with me?" she asked, cradling my face between her hands, holding me ever so slightly away from her, knowing as only a woman can know that the temptations she had thrown in my righteous path were having the desired effect. Then, almost desperately, as if she were giving me the key to enter paradise, she asked again, "Won't you say you're in love with me now?"

I understood what I had to do. How could I not say the words she wanted to hear? Although I had my principles, I realized that she had her principles too and that the act of sex meant nothing to her unless she felt loved. Why not be gallant and let her have her way? After all, wasn't gallantry also a principled characteristic? It was a small price to pay and one that was unavoidable in this instance. "Yes, I am in love with you, Emma Lou," I said. "I really am in love with you."

She began almost frantically to remove my shirt while I pulled her panties down her legs. She kissed my face and chest and legs; a little lie wasn't so bad after all.

"I am in love with you, Emma Lou," I said without reservation, lost helplessly in the passion and sin of the moment.

Suddenly, the words I had just spoken echoed in my brain, and I realized I really did love her; she, her mother, and her sisters meant a great deal to me, and I was not going to lie to her. The better angel in me took over, and I reached for her and helped her sit up against the head board. Then I retrieved my shirt from the floor beside the bed.

"What are you doing?" she asked, apparently confused by my unexpected behavior. It was obvious that she had never been turned down before, especially at the brink of consummation.

"I'm going downstairs."

"Don't you want to make love to me?"

"I sure do," I said, "but I'm not going to lie to you. I'm not in love with you, Emma Lou, and I shouldn't tell you that I am just to get you to have sex with me." By then I was standing in my undershorts and buttoning my shirt.

Smiling, and obviously touched, she said, "Jeff Stone, that is the sweetest thing anyone has ever done for me. Please don't go; I know you care about me more than all those other boys who told me they were in love with me."

"Then don't expect me to lie to you just to go to bed with you. I care too much about you to do that."

"You are so sweet," she said, "I want you to make love to me now."

"But I'm not in love with you; I probably won't ever be."

"It doesn't matter," she said. "I want you to make love to me anyway."

I smiled at her and stopped buttoning my shirt. She sat on the edge of the bed and extended her hand. I took it in mine and knelt on the floor in front of her. We kissed. I slowly moved onto the bed. As I felt the warmth of her body against mine and looked down into her dark brown eyes, I could hardly resist saying, "I'm in love with you, Emma Lou."

Coal Dust

E ach morning when my father kissed my mother good-bye and walked the half-mile trip to the company bathhouse where he changed into his mining clothes, we knew it might be the last time we would see him alive. Coal mining was fraught with danger for men who toiled amidst the choking black dust miles inside the mountains of Appalachia. It was a danger that filled me with both fear and fascination: a fear that the next anguished signal from the coal company emergency steam whistle would portend the death of my father; a fascination that lured me to see for myself the places under the mountain that fomented that fear.

By the time I was fifteen, I had grown bold enough to venture a mile or more inside the mine. My boldness was bolstered by my constant companion, Leroy Miller, who was my age and as mischievous and curious as I. His father also worked in the mine. Our curiosity had taken us far into the mountain along the main tunnel tram track, each time venturing a little farther to the worked out areas of the mine; these were the areas where no coal remained for the digging. They were dark, damp, dangerous, and well suited for conjuring the ghosts of the many miners who had perished inside the mine from rockfalls, cave-ins, and methane gas explosions.

I can recall all our forays under the mountain and can recount the details of the discoveries we made each time. They are all familiar to me but none more so than our final venture into the mine.

Leroy and I had reached the end of an unlighted section that branched off the main line. His flashlight—the one he had taken without permission from his stepmother—gave off a faint yellow ray that he trained on the mine floor as we made our way back toward the main line. Whispers from the ghosts of dead miners at our backs kept us moving at a slow, steady pace that belied my desire to run full speed in a direction that would lead us to light.

By the time we reached the entrance tunnel, the change of shifts had begun. The first tram carrying workers out of the mine had unloaded its blackened riders; they were streaming in twos and threes toward the mine entrance. Leroy and I hid behind the timbers that lined the sides of the tunnel and watched as they passed.

At the end of their shifts, black men and white men were walking together, covered with coal dust from head to toe. About all we could see were the whites of their eyes as they came through the tunnel. The miner's lamps mounted on the front of their safety caps shone ahead of them, beams flying randomly through the semidarkness with each stride.

The air was heavy with the coal dust and black powder that rose continuously from the tunnel floor, reenergized with each miner's tread; after reaching the roof of the tunnel, the particles drifted slowly back to the floor. The beams from the miners' lamps illuminated the shimmering black mist collapsing around them as they made their way toward daylight.

A large group of men passed by us, walking two and three abreast almost in unison. One man walked alone behind the procession, as if ostracized by the group. Just before he passed us, the figures of three large men with their lamps extinguished emerged from the darkness. They surrounded the lone man, preventing him from moving forward. The four remained stationary while the main group proceeded in the direction of the mine entrance.

We heard one of the instigators speak. "We want to talk with you, Epps."

"'Bout what?" we heard the lone man ask.

"You know what about, nigger," the first man said.

"Yeah," a second voice added, "we want to talk to you 'bout that white girl you been fuckin'.'"

"That's my daddy," Leroy whispered to me. He put his arm around my shoulder, and we listened even more intently.

"Don't know what you talkin 'bout," the captive miner said. "Don't know what the fuck you talkin 'bout."

"Rosella Collins, that's who we're talkin 'bout," Leroy's father said.

The third man, who was so tall that he had to bend his neck slightly under the tunnel roof, added, "We're warnin' you to stay away from her before you get into real trouble."

Leroy's father spoke again, sounding more reasonable than the other two inquisitors, "Look, Epps, you don't want to cause trouble for your daddy, do you?"

"It's Charlie Epps," I whispered to Leroy, nudging him with my elbow. "His daddy has the candy store up in Improvement Branch."

Leroy didn't say anything, just clasped my shoulder tighter. We watched and listened, afraid to make too much sound for fear of being discovered.

Charlie Epps made an attempt to walk away from his captors, but the big man grabbed him from behind and locked his arms around his neck and head.

"You been fuckin' that white girl, ain't you now?" the second man said, "Fuckin' her while Dewey is away in Korea; that ain't right."

"Man, I don't know what you talkin' 'bout," Charlie Epps said, his voice rising in pitch. "I done told you, I don't know."

"Bullshit," Leroy's dad said. "We know what's been goin' on; we're just tryin' to prevent trouble for you and your daddy." He paused for a moment, then added, "Dewey will be comin' home soon and somebody is goin' to get hurt when he finds out what's been goin' on."

"What the fuck you sayin'?" Epps protested.

"You better get your black ass out of Harlan County—that's what we're sayin'," the third man answered, talking directly into Epps's ear. "You better leave before the weekend is over."

"I ain't done nothin', and I ain't goin' no place," Epps replied.

The big man pulled Epps's arms behind his back and held them together with one hand as he yanked Epps's head back with his forearm, causing the victim's safety helmet to fly off his head. It dangled near the ground, its lamp still attached to his side by the battery cord hanging from his belt. The second man hit Epps across the face with his elbow.

Epps cried out in pain. He pulled himself free from the big man and ran in the direction of the mine entrance. The three men pursued and overtook him. The big man wrestled Epps to the ground and kicked him in his side. Epps lay groaning no more than thirty feet from us. "Please, I ain't done nothin' with no Rosella Collins."

"Bullshit," Leroy's dad said. "We know you been fuckin' that girl, and we're not goin' to stand for it; get our message?"

Epps sat up and then crawled quickly on his hands and knees away from the men. He began to run back in our direction before he had risen to his full height. The big man ran after him, tackling him hard. His head landed with a dull thud against one of the support timbers, where he fell just ten feet away from our hideaway. He didn't move.

Leroy's dad ran to the still body and bent over him. "Epps," he said, "Epps … Epps."

The big man rose to his knees and shook Epps by the shoulders. "Wake up, you nigger bastard. Ain't nothin' wrong with you. Wake up."

"Damn, I think you've killed him," Leroy's dad said.

"No, I couldn't have," the big man said, "I didn't tackle him that hard."

"Let's get the hell out of here," suggested the second man.

"Wait a minute," the big man said. "It's gotta look better than this." He put his shoulder against the support timber that Epps's head had struck and pushed until it fell across the supine man's chest. The overhead slate creaked; small pieces of debris fell from the tunnel roof, landing all around Epps. Coal dust swirled then settled on his body.

The three men gathered their lunch buckets and safety hats and walked swiftly toward the mine entrance. We watched as they marched away from us, their silhouettes slowly blending into the dark shadows of the tunnel. For several minutes, neither Leroy nor I dared to move. Finally, we crawled from our hiding place. Charlie Epps lay sprawled, face up, with the timber and pieces of slate across his chest. His safety helmet lay next to him, its lamp shining, illuminating the tunnel ceiling. We approached him to get a better look.

Black dust shimmered in the beam of the light like fine rain as it fell over the face of Charlie Epps. Standing there, it was impossible to tell whether he was black or white, but we knew with certainty.

Leroy and I ran headlong toward the blessed light that awaited us up ahead. Once outside, we kept running until we reached the gondola yard where coal cars, filled with the coal our fathers had mined the day before, awaited shipping. We sat on the ground between two rows of gondolas, looking at each other in disbelief, neither of us speaking. A few minutes later we heard the shrill steam whistle announcing that the body of Charlie Epps had been found.

Wages of Sin

Maria was a good-looking woman, about twenty-six, dark-haired, buxom, vivacious, and deliciously wicked. She wore tight-fitting, short skirts with white blouses. And she always had a wink in her eye. When she visited Sam's Market, where I worked as a stock and delivery boy, she would sit on a stool behind the counter, laughing and joking with Sam and me, with her skirt three or four inches above her knees, just enough to show the seductive curve of her thighs. She was very attractive atop that stool, especially when she crossed and uncrossed her legs, almost revealing the black bikini panties I imagined she was wearing.

Her apartment was on McMechen Street, a half block away from the store. Up two flights of stairs, the second apartment on the right was her three-room flat; it usually took me ten minutes to walk from the store, down the street, and up the stairs to her apartment. There came a time, though, when I could make the trip more quickly—that was after I got the idea that Maria would not be in a hurry for me to leave after I had delivered her groceries.

Sam's Market was located in a small building adjacent to a liquor store and across the street from the only drugstore within five city blocks. We sold meats, vegetables, canned items, baked goods, and dairy products. Most of our customers were long-established residents who lived within a couple of blocks of the store. Maria was one of the newer customers who populated the many old tenement buildings in our neighborhood for short durations. She showed up one day in the store and began talking to Sam, flirting with him as if she had known him forever. Within a few weeks, she had become a regular customer.

Most people probably would have considered Maria's conduct to be outrageous, but not Sam. He seemed to enjoy the breaks that Maria provided from the grocer's humdrum routine. Although it was pretty obvious that she was accustomed to using her good looks to get almost anything she wanted from men, I don't believe it ever worked with Sam. I wish I could say the same about myself.

When Maria learned she had the power to embarrass me to the point of blushing, there was no end to her kidding and cajoling. Nearly always, her final act before leaving the store was to pretend to proposition me. Once, she raised her skirt to the top of her thighs and asked, "Have you ever seen anything this good, sweetheart?" I didn't tell her yes or no; but in truth, I had never seen anything that made me lose my breath the way that did, at least, not very many times.

One Saturday morning, Maria called the store and ordered just enough groceries to fill a large grocery bag. I eagerly anticipated seeing her as I crossed the park and wound my way up the stairs to her apartment. When I rang the bell, she came to the door wearing a short black skirt and a white blouse unbuttoned to reveal the top of her strapless bra and the fullness of her breasts inside it.

I had come to think of myself as pretty worldly about women, and I had finally learned to hold my own with Maria in the store. But suddenly, alone with her in her apartment, I was again a sexual neophyte, thoroughly confused and intimidated by her obvious overtures.

I set the grocery bag on the table and handed Maria the bill. She pushed it down inside her bra without speaking. She placed one high heeled foot on the seat of a kitchen chair; this allowed her short skirt to slide back to reveal the tops of her thighs as she began slowly to remove all the items from the grocery bag, setting each of them ritualistically on the table. All the while, she smiled a slight smile and wet her lips over and over with her tongue, her dark eyes sparkling. She never spoke as she seduced me with those sensual eyes. The invitation was obvious, tempting, and so hard to resist, but after a few moments of silent equivocating, I forced myself to ask, in my deepest, most masculine voice and in my very best businesslike manner, "How do you want to pay the bill?"

"How much is it?" she teased.

"Ten something," I said.

"Don't you remember exactly, sweetheart?" Maria said, fingering the pencil that protruded from the top of my shirt pocket.

"No," I said, "you made me forget."

She laughed lustily, then picked up a box of margarine from the table and removed each stick one at a time, placing all of them on a small plate on the table. When she finished, she walked to the refrigerator and set the margarine inside. Next, holding open the refrigerator door with her knee, she opened the carton of eggs, and placed the eggs, all twelve of them, in individual egg holders inside the door. Maria then reached up to a shelf over the kitchen sink, stretching up as far as she could so that her skirt rose to reveal her underwear—which was white, not black as I had supposed—as she set three or four cans of food on the shelf. She picked up the loaf of bread and kneaded it softly with both hands before placing it gently in the bread box. Every move she made, I knew full well, was performed with deliberate intent to titillate. And I just stood there, helpless, holding the bottom of my white store apron knotted in my hands, wondering how I was going to get the money she owed me.

"I gotta get back to the store."

"Right now?" Maria asked, walking confidently around the table to stand facing me, her body two inches or less away from mine.

I understood better than I wanted to that Maria expected someone to pay for her groceries, and I hoped mightily it would not be me. I dropped the apron and attempted to find the words that would repel her, allow me to grab the money, and hightail it back to the store before I succumbed to her wiles. Instead, unfortunately, I put my arms around her waist and held her close enough for her to detect that she was winning the subtle negotiations taking place at her kitchen table.

"Aren't you curious about the exact amount of the bill?" she asked after a moment or two.

"Yeah," I said, shifting my weight from one foot to the other.

"Well, aren't you going to look at it?" she smiled seductively.

The notion of putting my hand on that suntanned, voluptuous breast paralyzed me, and for a moment, I stood like a statue, unable to speak or to move. She closed the distance between us and kissed me with an open mouth.

"Aren't you going to look?" she asked again, smiling, slowly blinking her eyes.

"Sure," I said mustering all the self-discipline I had remaining and stepping back dramatically. When I was a safe distance away from her, I held out my hand toward her defiantly and said, "Let me see."

For just a tiny moment, she looked less confident, perhaps even crestfallen, as I stood triumphant, towering above her like Ulysses. I had resisted the temptress. Her siren song had not lured me onto the rocks to be pounded mercilessly by the furious surf. Despite a mighty temptation, and very frankly, my own death wish in this regard, I had won. Though I might forevermore wonder about how it might have been with Maria, my stronger character had prevailed. I could now return to the store and proudly hand Sam ten dollars plus change, every penny Maria owed for her groceries. Seizing the moment, I thrust my hand in her direction, and with a great degree of authority, I said, almost pompously, "I have to go; let me see the bill."

She took my hand and held it momentarily as she looked at me through long, dark eyelashes; then smiling mischievously, she moved my hand slowly down under her bra, over her breast. "See for yourself," she said.

* * *

When I arrived back at the store nearly an hour later, I immediately busied myself behind the meat counter, straightening up the display, not looking at Sam or speaking to him. Then I began sweeping the floor, avoiding Sam's eyes, which I knew were watching me suspiciously. Normally, as soon as I returned, I would have given him the bill and the money that I had collected from Maria, but this time I didn't.

After a few long, uncomfortable moments, Sam asked, "Did Maria pay her bill?"

"What do you mean?"

"I mean did she send the money back with you?"

"No, she didn't," I said, "She didn't have any money."

"When does she plan to pay for her groceries?"

"I told her she could charge her groceries until Saturday and that I would lend her the money then to pay the store."

"When's she going to pay you back?"

"I don't know, but she told me she would."

Sam walked over to where I stood and placed his hand on my shoulder. "Are you sure that's the truth?" He was almost smiling, but I could tell he was not very pleased with me.

I couldn't compound one lie with another, especially not with Sam. "Not exactly," I said. "I gave her the groceries. But I told her I would let you take them out of my pay on Saturday."

"That won't leave you very much on payday."

"I know, but it's ok. I can get by this time."

"I hope that piece of ass was worth it," Sam said. He hesitated for a moment, then continued, "'Cause you aren't the first one to pay for her groceries."

"What do you mean?"

"I mean you aren't the first."

I didn't think he was talking about himself. But Sam was friends with several other grocers within a few blocks of our store; maybe he had heard something; maybe Maria had done the same thing with other delivery boys at other stores. I began to picture a dozen other guys going by Maria's apartment to drop off a bag or two of groceries. It made me think that I was probably one in a long line who had been unable to resist her. The thought that she might have even seduced Sam, and only God knew who else, suddenly stuck in my craw, and right then and there I made myself a promise that, no matter what she might do to entice me, I wouldn't let it happen to me again, that I was taking myself out of her grocery supply line for good.

My firm and resolute promise to myself remained inviolate for about a week, because it was that long before Maria came into the store again. She was wearing tight black shorts that barely covered her rear. They showed the complete curvature of her body, front and back.

She took a seat on the stool by the cash register. I busied myself behind the refrigerated meat counter, happy to feel the cool air flowing across my face each time I opened the sliding door to adjust the meat display. I would have stuck my head inside and remained there until I turned blue just to avoid Maria, but she had a whole lot more patience than I had resolve. Knowing that she was sitting there watching me, I couldn't resist sneaking a look at her every so often. With each glance, I feared more and more that I was doomed to be her love slave, buying her groceries probably forever, maybe having to ask Sam for a raise or more hours so I could keep her supplied.

When my nose and ears began to turn crisp from the cold, I rose from my bent position and looked in Maria's direction. She was watching my every move as I straightened my store apron.

"Hey there, lover," she said, smiling an all-knowing, all-telling smile.

"Hey there,"

"Why haven't you been to see me?"

"Did you want me to?" I asked as if the thought had never entered my young mind.

"Of course I did," she said, "Anytime."

Sam stood behind Maria, shaking his head from side to side. The message was obvious: "Boy, you can't afford this stuff, so forget about it and get your ass back to work."

I understood Sam's silent message and excused myself, glad that at least that he was one member of the male species who could keep his brain working even while all the blood in his system was rushing to another location in his body. How he could stand so close to Maria in her state of near undress and not feel what I was feeling was beyond my comprehension. I walked downstairs to the storeroom, which we always referred to as the dungeon, closed the door behind me, and sat on a box of canned tomatoes to contemplate ways to resist Maria.

I spent the next twenty minutes or so staring into space, slowly getting that bronze gypsy, who I knew was seated on the little round stool on the floor above me, out of my mind. After I regained my composure, I went back upstairs. My will reinforced by new reflections on good and evil, I was ready to take whatever she could dish out. But by then she had left the store.

I breathed a sigh of relief, grateful Maria was gone, but I knew that sooner or later I would have to face her again. And when I did, I hoped that I would be able to reject her. Still the question remained: would her next grocery order be paid out of my meager paycheck, or would I be able to resist the wicked enchantress the next time I found myself alone with her in her apartment? At that moment, there in the store, I had an impenetrable will to resist her. But whether or not I could hold up under fire, only God knew for sure. And He was quite willing to test my resolve and character one more time, even sooner than I could imagine: almost at that moment, Sam handed me Maria's short grocery list.

"She wants you to fill this order and deliver it about six this evening on your way home." Sam looked straight into my eyes; I knew he was searching for, at the very least, an implicit promise that I would not commit the same mistake I had made the last time I delivered groceries to Maria's apartment.

"Oh, God," I said to myself. I felt as if I had just emerged victorious from an arduous battle and let my guard down momentarily, only to be gunned down by a sniper's fire from a foxhole, just what happened to John Wayne in the movie *Sands of Iwo Jima*.

"Are you OK?" Sam asked, looking me up and down.

"Sure, I'm OK ," I responded, holding my hand over the gaping wound to my chest, only half-aware of his question.

I stuffed the grocery list in my shirt pocket and went about my chores for the next two hours. Occasionally my libido would overcome my iron will, and I would reread Maria's grocery list as if it were a love note from a secret admirer, then safely replace it in my pocket. As six o'clock approached, I began to anticipate what might be awaiting me on the third floor, second apartment on the right, of the building just down the street, across the park. I busied myself around the store, attempting to be productive, but I couldn't keep my mind off Maria. A few minutes before six, I put together her order, calling out the items to Sam while he totaled them on the cash register.

"Sixteen dollars and twenty cents," Sam said when I finished. "I'll give you change for a twenty to take with you."

"Good, then she won't have any excuse, will she?" I said, trying to sound very disinterested.

"No excuse in the world," Sam said, winking at me.

I walked across the park with a small box of groceries hoisted on my shoulder and strolled down the street and up two flights of stairs to Maria's apartment. I knocked and waited a moment or two until she opened the door. She was still in the black shorts she had worn to the store earlier that afternoon.

"Just put them on the table," she said, "and let me know what I owe you."

I didn't make the mistake of handing her the bill as I had done the last time I delivered groceries to her. Instead, I kept the paper and read the amount aloud.

"The damage is sixteen dollars and twenty cents."

As I extended my hand to be paid, she kissed me just as I was hoping and fearing she would. Instead of asking her for money, I began to undo the buttons on the front of her shorts, giving not one thought to Sam and how he might react or whether I would ever get paid for the groceries on the table beside me.

* * *

Repentance can come so quickly after sexual gratification, and men can divert their attention to business or other mundane matters as soon as the pleasures of sex have been attained; so it was for me that evening. After making love to Maria, the realization that I didn't have any money to give to Sam and that I wouldn't get paid anything on the next payday hit me. But it was too late to think about negotiating with Maria or how I would explain my failings to Sam the next morning.

Maria lay on the bed, propped up on her elbow, her chin resting in her hand, and looking as if she didn't have a care in the world; she probably didn't. But the world weighed heavily on my shoulders. In only a matter of moments, I had gone from emotional apogee to perigee, from elation to dejection, from gleeful sin to contrition. A verse from the Bible ran through my mind: "The wages of sin is death"; I thought how much better off I would be if I didn't live until tomorrow to face Sam. My saving grace was that at least I had the rest of the night to come up with some plausible explanation. While I dressed and contemplated my fate, Maria hummed contentedly.

"You were great," she said.

"You were too," I told her dejectedly without looking at her.

"You feel like doing it again?"

"Yeah, but I gotta get home," I said, tucking my shirt into my pants.

"You don't know what you're missing."

"Yeah, I do," I said, walking toward the door.

"See you later?"

"Yeah, see you later."

"Are you unhappy with me, lover?" she asked over my shoulder.

"No, but I'm unhappy with myself I guess," I said, turning my head just enough to see her face.

"You said you liked it; didn't you like it?"

"Sure, it was like nothing else I've ever experienced," I said, "but Sam will want to know what happened when I get to the store tomorrow, and—"

"Don't worry about Sam; tell him it's none of his damn business."

"We'll see."

"Don't worry now," she said, sitting up in bed, slipping her arms into a shirt.

"OK. Guess I oughta go." I turned back toward the door.

"Yeah, see you later, sweetheart," Maria said as I walked to the door. "How about tomorrow? See you tomorrow?"

"Maybe," I said, not feeling much comfort from her advice or assurances. Tomorrow, when I would have to tell Sam what happened with Maria, would come sooner than I wished; tomorrow, when I would have to explain why I didn't get any money from her, might be the day Sam would fire me. I had no idea what his reaction might be; if he did fire me, I really couldn't blame him.

When I looked at Maria now, she didn't appear nearly as enticing as she had a few moments earlier. She looked like a black widow spider propped up on her pillows, much older and more evil behind her broad smile and happy countenance than I had realized. She had used her experience to trap me in her web and inject me with poisonous venom that suffocated my will to resist. She had lain in wait for me, knowing I would become entangled once again; I had succumbed just as she planned. Perhaps it was too late to make amends to Sam, but I would try the next day; for now, it was enough to realize that I had learned a bitter lesson, and in the long term, I would be a better person for having had this encounter with Maria.

Just before I turned the doorknob, I looked back once more at her lying there, arms behind her head, still smiling. There was much I wanted to say, but nothing seemed right except, "See you, Maria."

"Oh," she said, "before you go, look on the table next to the door—there's a twenty dollar bill—and you can keep the change, lover."

I turned around to look at her, and I smiled.

"Maybe I can stay a little while longer," I said.

Let Us Entertain You

The Quinlin sisters, Eva and Anna, lived two blocks from Sam's Meat Market, where I worked when I was almost seventeen. Once each week, they bought their groceries at Sam's. Afterwards, they led the way back to their apartment while I carried a large box, filled with groceries, on my shoulder. We ascended their front steps, one sister walking ahead of me, the other following behind. At the top, I waited while they opened the large oak door and held it for me to enter.

"Just set the groceries on the dining room table, please," was my usual instruction from one of the women.

While they checked the contents of the box against their list, I stood quietly near the door, straightening my store apron and watching their ritual with some amusement. When they had verified their order, one of them would offer me a quarter tip, which I politely declined.

"Thank you, thank you," they would say, almost in unison, as I backed out the door.

Their apartment was dimly lit. Early twentieth century portraits hung in polished wood frames. Heavy drapes, once a deep green color but long since faded into shades of dusty gray, hung over the windows. Early American furniture and shaded lamps filled the rooms. Books, some several inches thick, many bound in heavy black or brown leather, lay stacked on tables. A large walnut rolltop desk sat against one wall, its cover open and its top neatly arranged. I assumed the furniture pieces were heirlooms from a once well-to-do family. This theory also explained how Eva and Anna subsisted, since apparently neither was employed.

The sisters were about forty years of age and close enough in appearance to be twins. They dressed impeccably, usually in black and white or black and gray. They were always moderately perfumed and wore just enough makeup to give the slightest hint of intrigue.

The Quinlins came to Sam's well prepared, with detailed grocery lists. From the precision and order in which they conducted their purchasing, I assumed they must have spent hours planning their shopping trip to Sam's Meat Market. One of them, usually Eva, read from the list while Anna took items off the shelf and put them into a shopping cart. She called out the price of each item. Eva entered the prices into a sandwich-sized calculator retrieved from her large handbag.

After all the canned goods, fruits, and vegetables were boxed, Sam cut meats, wrapped each item in butcher paper, and wrote the price on the wrapper with a number two pencil he kept over his right ear. He added all the prices in the cash register, but he never revealed his total until after the sisters announced theirs. After any differences were resolved, the sisters and I walked together to their apartment.

Eva and Anna appeared to live dignified and staid lives. There was an essence about them that made me believe they had grown up under strict moral and religious guidance. Their demure demeanors were suited to their subdued early American surroundings. I was in awe of the apparent sanctity of their apartment and was careful that my actions did not give any hint of irreverence. I spoke in hushed, courteous tones, which I believe endeared me to them.

Gradually, they began to reveal fragments of their lives. They took pride in the treasures that hung on their walls or lay hidden in the heavy drawers of the credenza and desk standing against the dining room walls. Their valuables included broaches, rings, necklaces, and bracelets. Several drawers held ostentatious costume jewelry, old letters, and photographs. Among their many books was a copy of *For Whom the Bell Tolls* personally autographed by Ernest Hemingway. Their most prized possession was a yellowed letter written to Mr. John Quinlin, Esq., their father, and signed by Adlai Stevenson.

One Saturday afternoon, when we were looking through old photographs and collectibles, Eva and Anna whispered to each other just out of my earshot. They both looked at me and smiled. After a moment, Anna said to Eva loudly enough for me to hear, "No, you ask him."

"Ask me what?"

"Do you like visiting us?" Anna asked.

"Yes, I do, very much."

"We're glad, because we enjoy your company."

Eva nodded in agreement.

"And I enjoy yours," I assured them.

"Would you like to visit more often?" Eva asked.

"Whenever you need me to deliver something for you?"

"Besides that, we mean."

"Sure, just let me know when."

With that issue settled, a lull fell over the conversation, and they sat quietly looking at each other, then at me. I cleared my throat and squirmed on my seat, trying to think of a gracious excuse for leaving. Just as I was rising to go, Eva placed her hand on my arm and inquired, "Do you have a girlfriend?"

"Nah," I lied, smiling and probably blushing.

"How about the pretty little blond girl that hangs out around the store?" Eva asked, reaching across the table to touch my hand. "Don't you like her a little?"

"You mean Susan Manning?" I asked as if I was completely disinterested.

"Yes, Susan, that's her name," Eva said, and to my surprise, added, "She lives in the fourteen hundred block of Eutaw."

"She isn't my girlfriend. She's just my best friend's sister," I said, attempting to make light of Eva's assertions. "She doesn't really like me. Anyway, she has brown hair, not blonde."

"Then why do you think she hangs around the store?" Anna asked.

"'Cause she doesn't have anything better to do," I said. "And she likes to talk to me."

"Well, if you don't have a girlfriend, why can't you be our boyfriend?" Eva asked.

"Sure," I said, going along with the obvious joke, "I'll be your boyfriend."

"Starting when?" Anna asked.

"Right now," I said, getting up from the table and pushing my chair back under it. "As of right now, I am, officially, your boyfriend."

I walked to the door with the ladies following at my heels. Anna reached around me to open the door. Holding it open, she looked into my eyes and with palpable sincerity said, "Remember, you're our boyfriend and not Susan's."

"Sure," I said, beginning to feel conflicted about the game we were playing, "I'm your boyfriend, yours and Eva's." But it occurred to me that I might have been wrong about the Quinlin Sisters and that they might be preparing to seduce me.

It is a fact that sixteen-year-old boys must brag about their conquests whether they are real, imagined, or overtly fabricated, and I was no exception. I needed to tell someone about the potential fulfillment of any boy's ultimate fantasy—sex with not one, but two attractive older women. But whom could I tell? Not Sam; he wouldn't believe me, and he might not allow me to deliver groceries to the Quinlins again. My best friend, Susan's brother? I couldn't risk the reputations of Eva and Anna or the possibility he might tell Susan. I had no one to confide in but my eighteen-year-old brother, whom I swore to secrecy.

"You are about to get your brains fucked out, sonny boy," Jason gleefully said. However, he probably believed I was imagining the whole thing, or else he would have insisted on a piece of the action for himself.

"I know," I said. "Isn't it great?"

During the next few days, I often mused about Eva and Anna. Each time Susan came to the store, I imagined the sisters peering through binoculars from behind their faded green drapery. I was always happy to see Susan, but coincidentally, I was concerned that her visits would jeopardize my chances for sex with the Quinlins.

The next weekend, the sisters came to the store, and I participated in the usual routine of selecting items and packaging them in a box. Afterward, I carried the box to their apartment. When all items had been placed in the refrigerator or on the cupboard shelves, Anna served tea. We sat around the big dining table sipping from our cups while talking about events of the past week. Without any deviation in her voice, Eva abruptly changed the subject.

"We saw you yesterday talking with that girl again." She looked for confirmation at Anna, who gave it with a slow nod of her head.

"What girl?" I asked, feeling as if I had been caught misbehaving.

"That girl we talked about last week," Anna said. "Susan, remember?"

"Oh, her? I guess I forgot," I said. "It just wasn't important." But I wondered what Susan would have thought of that denial. She probably would have snickered at seeing me in such an uncomfortable situation.

Eva spoke. "You said you were going to be our boyfriend. Didn't you mean it?"

"Sure," I said, "I'm your boyfriend and no one else's."

"Good," Eva said, "then we've got something we want to show you, but you can't ever tell anyone else. Is that a promise?"

"I promise," I said in eager anticipation of the sexual bliss that awaited me. I kissed two fingers and held them up in confirmation of my pledge.

"Thanks," Anna said, taking my hand in hers. She kissed the back of my fingers and smiled sweetly.

Eva got up from the table and walked to the window side of the room. Standing in front of the faded green drapes, she smiled broadly and removed the black vest she wore over a white long-sleeved silk blouse. Anna raised the lid of an antiquated record player on our side of the room and turned it on. She put an extended-play record on the turntable and said, "Listen."

As sounds of Natalie Wood singing "Let Me Entertain You" emanated from two speakers located somewhere behind the long curtains, Anna smiled. She began to move to the rhythm of the recording.

I sat silently, incapable of imagining what would happen next. Anna sat back down beside me to watch while Eva danced gracefully in front of the draped windows. She slowly removed her white silk blouse, revealing two full breasts held erect by a white bra trimmed in lace. She continued to move easily while she unbuttoned her skirt, which she let slide down her legs to the carpet. As she stepped out of her clothing, I suddenly had doubts about my prowess as a lothario, especially with two older, experienced women. I pushed back my chair and stood, ready to leave the room.

"I need to go," I said to Anna. By then, I had been away from the store for nearly an hour. I didn't really wish to leave but thought my offer to go might obviate my exposure to the sisters as a sexual neophyte.

Anna touched my arm and looked up at me disapprovingly. "Please don't go; Eva would be so disappointed."

I sat back down and watched Eva as she stood in her undergarments. She wore long, dark stockings, held on her milky white thighs by black-and-red garters. She seated herself on a chair after pulling it away from the table and seductively removed her stockings one at a time. Then, holding each one above her head, she let them slip out of her hand and glide freely to the floor. Moving with precision to the music, she appeared to be oblivious to the presence of Anna and me. Eva reached behind her back and unfastened her bra. She smiled alluringly as she pulled her arms free. She dropped the bra to the floor and revealed her bare-breasted form to us from across the table.

I shifted anxiously on my chair. Anna's hand lay across my arm, providing reassurance, making certain I had no notion to leave. By then, I was absorbed in the show, and was anticipating once again the sex that awaited me. My brother's gleeful encouragement resurfaced: "You are about to get your brains fucked out, sonny boy."

Amen, and wouldn't he feel like a dumb ass when he heard all about it?

The music ended, and the needle moved across the record to start the next song. Anna got up from the table quickly and reset the needle. Once again, strains of "Let Me Entertain You" began to play. Eva positioned herself across the table in front of me, and then slowly pulled down her panties. She smiled shyly as she stepped out of the lingerie and raised it to her eye level. She stretched the elastic band, pointing in my direction, and let go. The panties landed on the table just a few inches in front of me. Eva stood fully nude, wearing only her high heels. She bowed dramatically with an exaggerated sweep of her arm.

"Wow!" I said.

With that, Anna began to applaud, and I followed suit. Eva smiled confidently, obviously satisfied that she had performed well. I began to clap as loudly as I could.

"Wow!" I said again. "That was great."

I eagerly awaited whatever might happen next.

Eva gathered her clothing. Holding her hands over her breasts demurely, she walked quickly out of the room while the music continued to play. I watched her round, white derrière until she disappeared through the bedroom doorway.

Anna turned off the record player.

"Did you like that?" she asked, looking back over her shoulder at me.

"I sure did. It was great. Eva's beautiful."

"Whose boyfriend are you now?"

"I'm your boyfriend, yours and Eva's," I said enthusiastically, edging my way toward the bedroom where Eva had gone.

When I reached the bedroom door, Anna pulled on my sleeve. "You can't go in there."

"What do you mean?"

"You can't go in there. We don't allow men in our bedroom."

"Then what was that all about? That thing that Eva did … the dance?"

"It was a dance, just a dance."

"And what was I supposed to think about it?" I asked. "Didn't you believe it would cause me problems?"

"I don't know why it should have."

"Didn't you think it would, you know … excite me?"

"You have to learn to appreciate an artist's work for what it is."

"I don't understand," I said. "An artist?"

"Yes, an artist in the mold of Gypsy Rose Lee. Haven't you ever heard of her?"

"But I thought you were trying to stimulate me," I said, grasping for a delicate way to let her know I was sexually aroused.

"We didn't mean anything by it. We like you, and we just wanted to entertain you," she said, "to do something special for you."

"And nothing else?"

"Nothing else."

"Alright," I said, embarrassed and thoroughly frustrated. I straightened my apron and took a step toward the front door.

"Wait a minute," Anna said.

She walked quickly out of the room. She and Eva returned in a few moments, carrying a life-sized cardboard depiction of two young women, which they stood on the floor in front of me. There on the poster were the Quinlin sisters outfitted in tasseled bras, shorts, and black net stockings. The poster read

"EVA AND ANNA, The TWINLIN QUINLINS, Burlesque's Most Sophisticated Entertainers."

I looked at the poster, realizing how special the sisters considered me. I put my arms around Anna and then Eva and kissed each of them on the cheek. Then I walked to the door.

"I'm your boyfriend," I said with sincere humility.

As I opened the door to leave, Anna said, "The next time you come, it's my turn to dance for you."

The Thin Veneer

I met Gayle Mattingly the first week after I began working at Sam's Meat Market. She was a strikingly beautiful black woman in her midthirties. She was divorced and lived with her mother in an apartment just around the corner from Sam's, where I was a stockroom and delivery boy. She taught history at Roosevelt High, one of the segregated black schools in Baltimore. Every Saturday morning almost without fail, she would call the store and ask that I "bring around" her order. We quickly became good friends, and I looked forward to her Saturday morning phone calls and my visits to her apartment on Madison Avenue.

In the weeks that followed, our friendship grew. She loaned books to me, and often cut out newspaper or magazine articles for me to read. Many of them explored issues of segregation and race relations, especially items about Dr. Martin Luther King Jr. I discovered that Mark Twain, my favorite author, was one of her favorites. And from her I learned to truly appreciate his writings, as she explained to me how he used humor to ridicule the institution of slavery in America.

While Mrs. Mattingly and I talked, her mother, an old woman of nearly seventy, sat in a rocking chair across the room, knitting or crocheting. Sometimes I caught her looking suspiciously at me above her glasses as if she could see right through my thin veneer of racial tolerance. I was conscious of her watching me, and sometimes, when our eyes met, I would feel as if I had been caught red-handed feeling superior and condescending. And I wanted to say, "You're wrong, ma'am; you're wrong." Instead, I would just close my eyes and wait for the moment to pass. Mrs. Mattingly, sensing my uneasiness, would say something to make me laugh; when I did, her mother would laugh too. Then, having recognized her minor victory, she would begin to rock knowingly in her chair. The laughter made everything alright, and I would momentarily forget about her and carry on my conversations with Mrs. Mattingly as if her mother wasn't even in the room.

On one of the occasions after her mother had silently expressed her disapproval of me, Mrs. Mattingly walked with me to the kitchen door; as I was leaving, she put her arms around me and kissed me gently on the forehead. "Don't worry about Mother, Tommy," she said, "She has forgotten how to trust people, but I haven't yet." For several days, I thought about that kiss and the fragrance of her perfume, and I knew I was falling in love with Mrs. Mattingly.

Only one city block separated two very different worlds. Eutaw Place, where I lived, was populated with poor white families expatriated from the coalfields of West Virginia, eastern Kentucky, and Tennessee seeking a means of survival after the collapse of the coal mining industry. Working-class blacks lived on Madison Avenue, most of them having migrated from Alabama, Mississippi, and Tennessee to escape racial intolerance. They had slowly displaced the wealthy German and Jewish families that once lived on Madison Avenue. The segregation they had left behind in Alabama, Mississippi and Tennessee had followed them into the neighborhoods of Baltimore. The stretch of McMechen Street between Eutaw Place and Madison buffered these two worlds and served to meld their diversities. In addition to Sam's Meat Market, there was a drugstore, a small hamburger joint, and a liquor store, all catering to an integrated clientele. Yet there was a willful separation of the races: Eutaw Place was for whites; Madison Avenue was for Negroes.

I soon became aware of societal changes that were occurring all across the country. In many ways racial barriers were being slowly dismantled in cities like Baltimore. But I realized that the de facto segregation of the city was worse than the government-sanctioned segregation I had witnessed growing up in the South. The differences between the two races mattered much more in the city than they ever had in the small Kentucky community where I had lived. I quickly learned the epithets each race had for the other, but I made a sincere effort not to let them become part of my vocabulary. As my relationship with Mrs. Mattingly grew, it was very important to me that I would never say anything that would be offensive to her. As for Mrs. Mattingly's mother, I was determined she would eventually see how genuine I was and that she would learn to accept me the way Mrs. Mattingly did.

My Saturday morning deliveries to Mrs. Mattingly continued for several months. At about ten o'clock in the morning, I would take her order, fill two grocery bags, and carry them the block and a half to her apartment on Madison Avenue. I would walk past a dozen or more sets of whitewashed marble steps until I arrived at her apartment building. Then I would climb to the top of the stoop, ring the doorbell and wait for the buzzer that signaled me to enter. I would push open the heavy oak door with my shoulder and step inside the hallway. Soon the door to Mrs. Mattingly's apartment at the top of the stairs would open, and she would smile down at me, motioning with her hand for me to come upstairs.

One Saturday morning when I rounded the corner onto Madison, a group of black teenagers played on the sidewalk a few doors down from Mrs. Mattingly's apartment. Several older boys stood against the building; others were wrestling and pushing each other around on the pavement, preventing anyone from passing them. As I approached, they turned to face me. They said nothing, but they stood their ground. As I attempted to walk between two of them, the tallest boy shoved me, nearly causing me to drop the grocery bags. Two others stepped in front of me to block my way.

"Excuse me, fellows," I said. "I want to take Mrs. Mattingly's groceries up to her."

"Hey, honky, I ain't your fellow," one of the boys said.

"I don't want any trouble," I said cautiously. "Come on, guys, let me through."

"An' I ain't your guy, neither," the same boy said, looking around at the others and laughing.

"Yeah, look—he's scaret," another one said. "He's so scaret he's shitting his pants."

"I don't want trouble," I said.

I continued to move forward toward Mrs. Mattingly's apartment building, nudging the gang along with me, all the while looking up at her window. I hoped she would see what was happening and come to my rescue. When I finally reached the steps leading up to her apartment building, two of the boys climbed up ahead of me and blocked my way.

"Come on, guys," I said, showing my irritation. "Get out of my way."

The tallest boy suddenly pulled one of the grocery bags from my grasp, dumping its contents onto the sidewalk. I immediately dropped the other bag and hit the boy closest to me with my fist. Suddenly, I was knocked backward down the steps. As I fell, I grabbed the front of a boy's shirt, pulling him down with me. He landed on top of me on the sidewalk. I felt my legs and sides being kicked by one of my tormentors. I struggled to my feet, swinging wildly at anyone near enough to strike.

"You black bastards!" I yelled, as if I had said the same thing a thousand times before. The words came naturally; they felt righteous and therapeutic as I resorted to my basest instincts for survival.

I felt something smash against my skull, and I fell, dazed, onto the sidewalk. Through a mental fog, I knew I was being held down, and I thought I was going to lose consciousness. Suddenly,

I realized the gang was gone. I sat up and watched as they ran up the street and around the corner.

"You black bastards!" I yelled after them through my outrage, tears, and blood. "You black bastards." I began to sob. I turned to see Mrs. Mattingly standing by the steps. I knew she had heard everything I said, and I was ashamed.

She took my hand, and without speaking, helped me to my feet. Silently, we began to pick up the groceries and put them back into the bags. Afterward, she opened the front door and I followed her up the stairs to her apartment, all the while wondering how I could ever explain to her why I had said the things I had. I wondered how she would have reacted—and probably had reacted—to similar situations. I knew that no matter the circumstances, she would not have succumbed to the same temptation as I; rather, she would have resisted with a dignity cultivated under difficult social circumstances, a dignity that I obviously did not possess. I was certain our friendship could never be the same again with her knowledge of what a bigot I really was.

We set the groceries on the kitchen table, and she told me to remove my shirt and have a seat. She wiped the blood from my face and neck with a washcloth. After she had finished, she bent down and kissed me gently on the forehead. Tears filled my eyes. I put my arms around her waist and buried my head against her perfumed midriff. "I'm so sorry," I said. "I'm so sorry. I wish to God I hadn't said what I did. I really didn't mean it."

Removing my arms from her waist, she said, "You had a right to say whatever you wanted to say. I know you very well, and I know that you did nothing to provoke those boys."

"I didn't," I assured her, looking up into her dark eyes as she bent over me, inspecting my face for more cuts and bruises, "but I shouldn't have said the things I said."

Mrs. Mattingly pulled another chair away from the kitchen table and sat on the edge of it directly in front of me. "I don't blame you in the least, but I just want to make sure you understand yourself as well as you think you do, Tommy."

"What do you mean?"

"What I am going to ask you doesn't matter as much to me as it should to you; so I want you to think about it before you answer. I want you to be true to yourself."

"I will," I promised, wondering what she was talking about.

"Would you have regretted saying what you did if I had not heard?"

I thought about it for a minute or two, then answered," I don't know." I lowered my eyes to the floor in front of her.

"Think about it," Mrs. Mattingly said as she stood up. She pushed her chair back under the table, turned to the kitchen sink, and began wiping pots and pans and stowing them in the overhead cabinets.

I thought about her question for several minutes. I realized she had hit upon the truth about me—that I had prejudices just like other people did and that I had reacted like almost anyone else would have. But I realized that while trying to fight back at the ones who had hurt me, I had hurt Mrs. Mattingly, someone I cared deeply about. In my anger and confusion, I did not feel any regret or remorse for my words. And I was at a loss to explain my feelings to her. Then it occurred to me that I would have reacted the same way if I had been attacked by a gang of white boys. I would have flailed at them physically and verbally, saying whatever I thought would hurt most, be the most cutting.

I wondered how many similar encounters would take place in the city that day, all motivated by race; in more of those instances than not, blacks would suffer berating attacks by whites. I abhorred my participation in the incident in front of Mrs. Mattingly's apartment, but I could not say I regretted what I had said to the gang that attacked me. Finally, I rose and stood behind Mrs. Mattingly. I spoke as honestly as I could, projecting the words to her from over her shoulder. "I'm sorry if I hurt you, but I'm not sorry for what I said."

"I know, and I appreciate your honesty; but don't you think you helped make the case for those boys?" she asked, turning to look at me.

"What do you mean?"

"I mean do you understand that you made them feel justified for what they did to you?"

"How did I do that?" I asked. "I didn't do or say anything to them."

"Tommy, everything each of us does individually is representative of society as a whole. Those boys had nothing against you personally. They simply see you as a part of the white establishment that keeps them from advancing and so they attacked you. You proved them right by calling them the names you did."

She hesitated, and then put her hand gently on the side of my face. "Let me ask you something."

"Go ahead."

"Do you think a black boy could work for Sam?"

I shook my head. "No."

"And if he could, could he deliver groceries in a white neighborhood without being attacked sometime or other?"

"I never thought about that."

"It's time you do," she said, handing me my shirt. "And when you do, I'm sure you will come to understand their resentment. Although you view yourself as being poor, you have much that those boys envy. Most of all they envy your freedom and your access to a society they can only see from the outside looking in. They have no right to anything you own, and they have no right to hurt you, but I want you to understand why they feel as they do."

I put on my shirt. She took my hand and led me to the living room. We seated ourselves on a sofa across from her mother. Nothing more was said by either of us for a long time. Mrs. Mattingly took a Bible off the table next to her and removed from between its pages a newspaper article, which she handed to me. It was a picture of Martin Luther King Jr. making his famous speech in front of the Lincoln Memorial.

"One day," she said, as she handed the picture to me, "it won't matter what color we are, but it matters now to many people."

"I don't think it matters to me, but I don't regret what I said to those boys."

"I understand," she said, "but maybe you will come to regret the things you said so easily and can change the way you really feel … and maybe someday I can change the way I feel also."

"What do you mean?" I asked, worried that she might decide to end our friendship.

"I mean that I have to work hard every day to overcome my prejudices too."

"You?" I asked incredulously.

"Yes, me too," she said, and then she paused for several seconds, obviously choosing her words carefully. "You and I are not like most people. We really don't want to be prejudiced, but there is so much of it around us, we get caught up in it. Circumstances make us prejudiced; the way we are forced to live and associate makes us prejudiced. We just have to try hard not to be so wrongly influenced by our circumstances."

"You?" I asked again, finding it difficult to understand that this gracious woman could feel prejudice toward anything or anyone.

"Me too," she smiled as she put her hand on my arm. "But I am your friend, and you are my dear friend. Friends should be able to talk about their differences. Our friendship shouldn't end because one of us makes a mistake or because we are honest with each other—we have shared too many wonderful times to let that happen. And we care too much about each other; don't you know that?"

I felt reassured sitting next to her and moved closer to her on the sofa to let her know I was comfortable with the things she was saying. I lowered my eyes to the newspaper article and began to read the words she had underlined there: "the content of one's character ..." I felt I realized exactly what Dr. King had meant that day, and I knew then that the kind of character he was speaking of was embodied perfectly in Mrs. Mattingly. I felt wonderful for a few shining moments, and I was certain that my contentment glowed.

I looked up from the paper and directed my gaze across the room to where Mrs. Mattingly's mother sat rocking. The old lady watched me knowingly above her glasses as she continued knitting and smiling.

A Dangerous Woman

Rita Smith lived alone in her second-floor apartment after her husband, Stewart, left her for another woman.

My family lived in a tenement only a few doors down. I sometimes delivered groceries to Miss Rita from Sam's Market where I worked, located just around the corner. On summer evenings, she and her friends, like most of the women who lived on our block, sat on the white marble steps leading from the street to their apartment building. There, they solved the problems of the world and passed on to each other the most recent snippets of gossip they acquired each day.

Sometimes, on my way home after helping Sam close up the store, I would stop to sit and hear the latest rumors. It was not unusual for the conversation to get around to the cost of living, Sam's Market, and *that goddamn Jew.* Sam and every other Jewish store owner in the neighborhood were fair fodder for Miss Rita and her friends, who had never experienced a dime saved beyond next payday. They envied anyone of more fortunate circumstance.

To Miss Rita and her friends, nothing was sacrosanct. Besides Sam's high prices, they included in their diatribes the hot weather, the noise in the city, and the war in Vietnam. Their conversations were often enlivened by sexual innuendo and thinly veiled assertions about their husbands and bedroom problems. Miss Rita's contributions to the giggling gaggle were by far the most entertaining and titillating, often detailing the latest attempts by someone to seduce her.

"Men are all the same," Rita would say, pausing for dramatic emphasis. "Lecherous bastards!" She would grind out her cigarette on the marble step, then key in on Sam just to make her point more poignant for my benefit. "Every time I go into the store, that goddamn Jew tries to feel me up."

I always defended Sam, because I knew that whatever she might say about him was more imagined than real. I would tell her that she misunderstood his attempts at goodwill. He always joked with his customers, especially flirtatious, attractive women. But she insisted that he was a cheap, horny Jew.

"He wants to get into my pants, but he's not going to." She would laugh, and then continue, "As much as he charges for his groceries, he can afford to pay whatever this stuff is worth, and believe me it's worth plenty." With that, she would slap herself on her nicely formed derrière for emphasis, bringing laughter from everyone.

One afternoon, when Sam and I were alone in the store, I spoke about Miss Rita and her friends. My boss busied himself behind the counter as I leaned on my broom and related some of my recent conversations with her. Sam's mischievous smile broadened as he opened the cash register. He broke open some rolls of change, dumped them into the register, and then closed the drawer. He didn't speak for several moments. Finally, he looked up from the register, and, sounding as serious as I had ever heard him, said "Boy, you've got a lot to learn about women. You had better watch yourself around Miss Rita—don't you know she is a dangerous woman?"

"What do you mean?" I asked, wondering if Sam was putting me on or if Miss Rita might have information about Sam that he'd prefer to keep concealed.

"She is a bitter woman," he said, "and a bitter woman is a dangerous woman. You never know what the hell they will do or say." He paused for a few moments, untied his apron, straightened the front of it, and then retied the strings behind his back—one of his habits when he was thinking. "I admit she is fine looking, but you don't want that kind of woman to know anything about your business or to have anything on you she can ever use against you in the wrong way."

"I think she's kind of nice," I said, "and she's funny; maybe she's a little uncouth at times, but she doesn't mean anything by it."

"She's a schlep."

I didn't know exactly what the Yiddish term meant, but I had heard Sam say it often enough to know it didn't mean anything good.

"No, she's not," I said. "She just doesn't have much money."

"Money doesn't have anything to do with it; she doesn't have much class."

"She's OK," I said, "and pretty."

"You're seventeen; what do you know about women?" He smiled again. "Your head is full of little pussies, and you can't think straight."

"I know enough." I straightened my shoulders and stood more erect.

"Yeah, you know just enough to get yourself into trouble."

By then, both Sam and I were laughing.

"You better be real careful what happens between you and Miss Rita," Sam said just before he walked into the meat locker, putting an end to our conversation.

A few days later, when I delivered Miss Rita's groceries, she told me that she had seen her landlord, Mr. Ladd, spying on her through her bathroom window. She insisted that I come into the bathroom so she could show me where he had stood on the fire escape adjacent to her window. I assumed the thought never entered her mind that I might be interested in seeing her in a state of undress or that I might climb up that same fire escape to get a look for myself after she had, by way of illustration, shown me how easy it might be. And I am certain she never considered how very much the view of her bathroom from the fire escape might be curtailed by lowering the blind or closing the curtains over her window completely.

After that, her conversations got more personal each time we were alone. When I delivered her groceries, she would keep me in her apartment as long as possible while she unpacked the items and checked them against her list. She would talk about her past love life with her husband and how she had done everything she could to satisfy him, to make him feel like a man. Sometimes, I thought she was inviting a pass from me, but I was too uncertain of her intentions to try finding out for sure. All the while, I thought of Sam and his warning.

"Do you know what a pervert is?" she asked one day during one of our conversations.

"I guess so," I said, "but I don't think I have ever known one."

"You'll know one when you meet one. There are all kinds of perverts. Some are men who prey on little boys or little girls; others are men who don't know how to have a normal relationship with a woman, so they do strange things. That's the most common kind of pervert."

"Is Stewart a pervert?"

"Judge for yourself," she said as she slowly opened the thin robe she was wearing and stood in nothing but her bra and panties. "He would have to be to run off and leave this, wouldn't he?"

I suddenly found myself paralyzed, unable to speak. I was afraid to look at her too long, fearing that I might turn into a pillar of salt if I faced her head-on. Excited and embarrassed, I diverted my eyes.

"Don't you like what you see?" she asked knowingly.

"Yes, ma'am, I do," I said, daring to look at her nicely shaped legs, then quickly moving my eyes back to the floor. Sam's caution rang in my ears: "Miss Rita is a dangerous woman."

"Well," she said, "don't you think a man would have to be a pervert to leave something this good?"

"It is hard to understand," I admitted, looking into her eyes as she put her arms around me and pushed her breasts against my chest.

She smiled and kissed me as she touched the bulge under my trousers.

Sam's caution sprang to mind again, and I attempted to push Rita away. "I've got to go," I said through a passionate kiss as she held me by my shoulders.

"You don't feel like you talk," she said as she kissed me and rubbed her hand on my penis through my pants.

She undid the top button of my trousers. I pushed her back and held her away while I caught my breath and cleared my head. "I have to go," I said, looking at my watch. "Sam's gonna fire me."

"That damn Jew will answer to me if he fires you," she said with a wink.

"I have to go," I said desperately with my last breath of resistance.

"You don't know what you're missing."

"Believe me, I do," I said. "I sure as heck do."

That made her smile; she let go of me, pulled her robe across her breasts, and tied the sash as she walked in front of me to the door.

"Are there any women perverts?" I asked, standing in the doorway, trembling and not wanting to leave but knowing I would no longer have a job with Sam if I didn't make my exit.

"No," she said, "women can't be perverts; they can only be horny."

"And are you horny?"

"Only for the right man," Rita said, winking again and patting me on the back of my shoulder just before she closed the door behind me.

When I returned to the store, Sam gave me a good once-over as I handed him Miss Rita's payment. I then walked the length of the store toward the back of the meat counter. In spite of my calm outward demeanor, I was certain he knew everything that had happened between Miss Rita and me.

"Where in the hell have you been?"

I picked up a broom and began to sweep behind the counter without speaking. The bristled instrument was my refuge in moments of crisis. Sweeping the floor had a therapeutic effect; it cleared the cobwebs from my brain.

"You've been gone forty-five minutes to deliver two little bags of groceries; isn't there some explanation?"

"She wouldn't let me leave, Sam," I said, "You know how she is, and she was having a crying jag, talking about her husband and all that."

"Yeah, I'll bet."

But I was sure he didn't believe a word I told him. I wondered how in the world Sam knew everything about everybody, how he had become so wise in only thirty-five years of living.

One week later, Miss Rita called the store to place an order. Sam took the call, and then handed the grocery list to me. As I picked the items off the shelves, I thought about what happened the last time I was in her apartment. I might have done the right thing by turning her down, but I had fantasized all week about what I missed out on. As I filled the grocery bags, knowing I was about to put myself at her mercy once again, I hoped and feared she would make another pass. I avoided looking at Sam, because as surely as I knew my name, he would read my mind.

"You deliver these groceries and get right back to the store," Sam said. "We're going to be busier than hell today, so you don't have time to entertain Miss Rita."

"Would you like for me to tell her that, Sam?" I asked jokingly.

"Yes," he smiled, "you tell her as soon as you get there."

I did my best to be calm right up to the moment I walked out of the store carrying two grocery bags in my arms. Then I walked as fast as I could toward Miss Rita's apartment.

She opened the door wearing her bathrobe; her hair was wet, and she had a towel around her shoulders. "Come on in," she said, closing the door quickly. She was clearly upset and in no mood for sexual banter. Apparently, something significant had occurred between the time she had called the store and my arrival at her apartment.

I put the grocery bags on the kitchen counter while cautiously watching Miss Rita. She paid me without checking their contents. That old saw about a woman scorned came to mind as I slipped her payment into my pocket and took a step toward the door to leave.

"Wait a minute. Don't go."

I turned to look at her; she was crying.

"What's wrong?" I asked.

"Can I trust you?"

"You know you can."

"I mean, can I really trust you?" she asked as she stepped closer to me.

"I guess so," I said, equivocating now as I recalled Sam's warning to me and wondering what deep, dark secret Miss Rita was about to lay upon my conscience.

"I have killed Jack Ladd," she said, the corners of her mouth turning down and more tears welling in her eyes.

"Miss Rita!" I exclaimed in disbelief, looking for some indication she was joking.

Instead, she leaned her head against my shoulder and began weeping quietly. I knew then it was not a joke. "How? Why?" I asked, bewildered. "When?"

"He was trying to hurt me; I hit him with my shoe … and he's on the bedroom floor. He's dead." She sobbed uncontrollably.

"Are you sure?" I asked, lifting her head to look into her face.

I could already see the evening headline: SLUMLORD KILLED WITH SHOE.

"Yes," she said tearfully.

"Why?"

Her weeping turned to anger. "The bastard was looking through my bathroom window again, and when I yelled at him, he forced his way into my apartment and into my bedroom. He tried to rape me; I hit him with my shoe." Then she said sadly, "He's dead; I've killed him."

The headline got more graphic: WOULD-BE RAPIST SLUMLORD DEAD, KILLED WITH TENANT'S SHOE.

"Let's call the police," I said, "We have to call the police."

"They won't believe me," she protested, sobbing.

"Sure they will—if it happened the way you say it did," I reassured her, knowing that no one could blame her for defending her honor.

She suddenly became hysterical. "It did! It happened just like I said. If you don't believe me, why would the police?"

"I believe you; they will too," I said, picking up the phone receiver. "I'm calling them."

"No, wait; we can't do that," she said, taking the phone from my hand.

I heard the word *we* and realized that things were getting more complicated than I wished. I might soon become complicit in a terrible crime. For a moment, I longed for Sam's sage advice. He would have known exactly what to do in a moment like this.

"I mean it didn't happen exactly like I said. There's more to it."

"Then tell me now," I insisted, "and maybe I can help you figure out what to do."

She sat on the sofa as I knelt on the floor in front of her, looking up into her face. I was doing the best I could to understand how she had gotten herself into such a mess. Tears ran down her cheeks as she continued talking. I wiped them away with my fingertips. She had me in the palm of her hand, ready to believe whatever fabrication she could invent. But truth is stranger than fiction and sometimes more twisted than the best of lies. Such was the story she, in her moment of desperation, revealed to me.

"Jack Ladd and I were lovers. That's why Stewart left me."

The headline exploded in bold print: LOVE TRIANGLE ENDS IN DEATH; TENANT KILLS SLUMLORD LOVER WITH SHOE.

"Lovers?" I asked in disbelief and disgust. "But I thought you didn't like for him to look at you."

"I didn't," Rita said, "but he took care of my rent; I didn't have to pay him a dime."

"Did Stewart know that?"

"Yes, Stewart knew about it and didn't care as long as the rent was paid and as long as I took care of him too."

"So what happened?" I asked, trying to understand but not really wanting to know the whole sorry mess.

"When Jack's visits got too frequent, Stewart wanted my relationship with him ended, but I couldn't do it. By then Stewart had been fired, and we didn't have any other way to pay the rent."

"Then why did you kill him?"

"I didn't mean to," she said. "I called Sam's to place my order and then took a shower while I waited for you to come over." She smiled through her tears, reaching out to run her fingers through my hair and caress my face— in short, doing her utmost to win my sympathy. "I had something good planned for you, but Jack came through the bathroom window and entered my bedroom; he wanted sex. I told him you would be here with my groceries any minute and that I wanted him to leave."

"Yeah?" I said, suddenly recognizing that I had completely underestimated my sex appeal to older ladies.

"He wouldn't leave," she said, "and we fought."

"Did he hurt you?" The side of me emerged that was the protector of helpless women. I was looking for justification—

anything to keep the innocent little lamb sitting on the couch in front of me out of jail.

"No," she continued, "I told him that I wasn't going to have sex with him anymore and that I was waiting for you to come with my groceries. He wanted to wait in the bedroom until after you had made the delivery, but I wouldn't let him stay."

Now that I understood my power over her, Miss Rita's story made perfect sense to me; I only needed a few more facts to completely understand how this defenseless but selfadmittedly horny woman had committed such a fatal act. "What happened then?" I inquired.

"I told him again I wanted him to leave because I didn't want him to be here when you came," she explained. "He became jealous and threatened to kill both of us."

Understanding her dilemma but wanting to let her down as gently as possible, I said, "Miss Rita, I like you a lot, but Mr. Ladd didn't have any reason to be jealous; I was not going to have sex with you. You know that, don't you?"

I think she was offended by my easy rejection of her—the second such rejection in only a two-week period. "Can you look at me now and honestly tell me you wouldn't make love to me if I offered?" she asked as she placed her hand gently on the side of my face.

Suddenly, her face glowed. Her countenance was clean from her recent shower and washed afresh with the tears she had cried. She was pretty and pure as twenty-four-karat gold; for a moment I could imagine Mr. Ladd wasn't dead on the bedroom floor, and I kissed her.

"Look at me," she said, untying her robe and pulling it aside. She wore nothing underneath. "You know, you really turn me on."

She put her hands on my shoulders and pulled me toward her, resting my face between her warm thighs. The temptation was overwhelming but still not strong enough to distract me from the image of the dead landlord lying on the floor of the back bedroom. An eerie vision of the death scene surged through my young mind one more time, and then Sam's words of wisdom, so presciently spoken just a few days earlier, coursed through my brain, warning me of clear and present danger. I trusted mightily that the force of such insight would overcome my growing desire to put my lips against Rita's warm little belly and that my carnal desires would be subjugated to more lofty ideals and to justice. I was confident that I would do the right thing. But it wasn't meant to be.

We made love on the sofa in the living room. When the act was over, the words spoken by Sam came back to me—"This woman is dangerous!"—and I knew with certainty that it was true. In a moment of weakness, I had let this dangerous woman make me an accomplice to murder.

A new headline flashed before me—the same one that would be on all the six o'clock TV news stories: GROCERY BOY ACCOMPLICE IN SLUMLORD MURDER, HELPED LOVER HIDE BODY.

I then resigned myself to the sorry task before me. "What do you want me to do, Miss Rita," I asked dejectedly.

"We've got to get rid of the body, don't we?"

"Yeah, I guess," I said. "Let's go see."

"You go," she said. "I can't bear to see him again."

"OK," I said, and walked toward the bedroom, dreading the bloody sight waiting there. Just then I heard a window slam shut, and I ran to the bathroom to look out. A tall, balding man was climbing down the fire escape. I ran to the bedroom. On a throw rug beside the bed were several small spots of blood, but Mr. Ladd was nowhere around.

* * *

When I returned to the store, I could see that Sam was angry, but I was so relieved not to be an accomplice to murder that Sam's anger could not possibly intimidate me. He took the money Miss Rita had paid me and placed it in the cash register drawer, which he then slammed shut.

"I ought to fire your ass," he said. "You have been gone for almost an hour."

"I'm sorry," I said, "but I was just helping out one of your customers."

"Yeah, I know," he said, "but I told you we would be very busy today."

"I tell you what," I said. "Why don't you deliver Miss Rita's groceries from now on, and I won't have to go around there again?"

"No," he said, "that woman is too dangerous."

"I know," I said, understanding exactly what Sam meant and wondering about the details of how he came to his own conclusion on the topic. "She is dangerous."

In Good Hands

There was no way they were going to make it through the remainder of the evening without an argument. Hell, we hadn't been in the bar more than twenty minutes before half the guys in the place were coming over to our table and asking Thelma to dance. Frank, he just sat there seething, drinking his beer slowly, watching every move she made on the dance floor. I had heard him tell Thelma, as they walked just ahead of me into the High Country bar, that she had better not dance with "every goddamn asshole in the place." When he started chugalugging his beer, I knew there was going to be hell to pay for someone and that we were all in for one raucous evening if I didn't intervene before things got too far out of hand. I had been in that same situation with Frank and Thelma too many times before not to be able to see what was coming if I didn't step in.

Frank was my best friend. We had been tight for more than a dozen years, and I couldn't begin to tell you all the things he had done for me during that time, especially since I divorced my second wife, Julie, and began living alone again. Thelma, well, she was Frank's third wife, a beauty several years younger than he. I guess I've never seen a woman with more allure; not only was she beautiful, but she was fun to be around—always laughing and wanting to have a good time. I don't want to say she was a flirt, but I guess that's the most appropriate way of putting it. Whenever a guy looked at her hungrily, she always smiled at him, communicating that she appreciated knowing he wanted to get into her pants. I suppose she just needed more attention than one man could supply, and I don't suppose Frank complimented her as frequently as all the other men out on the dance floor did. But I knew something those guys didn't—when the night was over, Thelma would without a doubt be going home with Frank. At least, that's how it had always been in the past.

Frank was a big man, nearly six and a half feet tall, and broad shouldered; not very many guys fucked with him, especially when he was drinking. But no sooner would Thelma sit down than another guy from across the room would make his way to our table, reaching out his hand at the same time Thelma raised herself out of her seat. Back to the dance floor she would go, swishing her midlength white gingham dress and clasping the barroom cowboy's arm. Why those guys wanted to risk Frank's ire by asking his wife to dance was puzzling to me, but I guess they just couldn't overlook Thelma's inviting smile. I suppose they thought that getting a chance to pull her tight little body up against theirs was worth the risk of getting their ass kicked by Frank. Anyway, that particular night, like a lot of others before them, Thelma's admirers kept feeding the jukebox and asking her to dance. And she danced with everyone who asked her.

Two dozen songs and two dozen dances later—about two dozen beers later for Frank—I could see that my friend had endured about all he could and that the next guy who approached our table might get a punch in the mouth. I thought I would do something to ease the situation. I excused myself to the bathroom, and on the way back I made it a point to pass close to the tables on the other side of the dance floor, where most of the guys who had been dancing with Thelma all night were sitting.

"How about taking it easy with Thelma? Let up on asking her to dance so much," I requested, directing my remarks in the general direction of the middle table. "Her husband is getting pissed off."

The king of the cowboys—resplendent in his red and black western shirt, tight Lee jeans, and pointy-toed black lizard boots—responded, "Fuck you, man; she wants to dance, I'll dance."

"And you might get your ass kicked too," I said.

"You?" one of the other guys sneered derisively.

"Not me," I quickly clarified, nodding my head in the direction of our table, "Frank, her husband—the big guy."

"Fuck him too," he said.

"Yeah, I'll let him know," I replied, half-smiling as I turned to walk back to our table.

I think the cowboys felt safe in numbers, and I really didn't expect that my caution would have much effect on them, but to my surprise the dance requests did stop for a while. In fact, at least three or four songs played on the jukebox without anyone asking Thelma to dance. Then I noticed the king—he had danced more with Thelma than anyone else—making his way toward our table.

"Wanna dance?" he asked, ignoring both Frank and me and looking directly at Thelma as if she were the only one present.

Thelma made an attempt to get up from the table. Frank placed his big hand on her arm. "Sit down," he instructed as he pushed his chair back and stood towering above the king by more than seven or eight inches. The king looked Frank up and down for a moment, then sauntered empty armed back to his own table.

I breathed a sigh of relief and sipped on my beer for awhile without speaking. Thelma and Frank sat in silence too. Finally I said—I suppose with naiveté, because I already knew what his response would be— "Why don't you dance with Thelma yourself, Frank?"

"Goddamn, Lenny, you know I don't dance; whyon't you dance with her?" By then, the beer had begun to affect Frank, slurring his already slow, bucolic speech. Frank hailed from somewhere up in the Georgia mountains, *Deliverance* country, and although he hadn't been back there in years, when he spoke he still sounded as if he had moved out only yesterday.

"Yeah, Lenny," Thelma said, taking my hand, "come on. You dance with me."

"You mind, Frank?" I asked cautiously. I had danced with Thelma many times before, and Frank never seemed to mind, but I had learned that when he was full of beer and ready to kick some ass, no one had better fuck around with his wife. "You mind if Thelma and I dance?"

Frank reached across the table and put his big hand on my arm. Almost crying, he said, "I'd trust you with my life, buddy. There ain't nothing I wouldn't trust you with, including my wife."

"Thanks, Frank," I said. "I hope you really mean that."

"You bet your ass, buddy," he said, gripping my arm with his humongous hand.

I just sat there looking at him and then at Thelma, overwhelmed, I suppose, by the trust he had in me and wondering if I really merited it. If the truth be known, there had been times when Thelma looked mighty damn good to me and times when I was not sure I could have turned her down if she had said the right thing or made the right move toward me. Thelma smiled sweetly, looking alternately at Frank and at me as he extolled my many virtues and praised my steadfast friendship.

"Thanks, Frank," I repeated a half-dozen more times before he and his beer quit talking.

Eventually, Thelma spoke up. "Come on, Lenny. Let's dance."

"Go on," Frank said, as Thelma and I started to move away from the table. He reached out and grabbed my hand, pulling me toward him so that my face was right in front of his for a moment. "There's one thing I know, buddy," he said. "When my woman is dancing with you, I know she is in good hands."

"You bet, Frank," I said. "You bet." I patted him on his big shoulder, and then turned back toward the dance floor, where Thelma by then stood waiting for me.

We put our money into the jukebox and danced to several songs in a row: "Boot Scootin' Boogie," "Ain't Got Nowhere to Go," something else, and then "I Will Always Love You." Thelma had laughed and moved around like crazy to all the fast tunes, but when the slower song started, she lost her grin, nestled her head up against my shoulder, and breathed soft, warm breaths against my ear. I could feel every tender, inviting inch of her pressing against me. She sighed every so often, just like a man wants a woman to do. As much as I liked having her close to me, I was relieved when the song ended, because I knew Frank was watching every move we made. I just didn't know how much longer I could stand her sweet-smelling form nestled up against me like that. When the song was over, I steered Thelma back toward our table, letting her walk on ahead so I could calm myself before Frank noticed the effect her nearness had provoked in me.

I stood there for a moment watching the smile that came across Frank's face as he pulled her chair out. It made me feel terrible and guilty as hell for having gotten worked up over Thelma. Frank loved her, and I knew it. She loved him too; it was just that she needed something more than he, or anyone else, could give her. I told myself that this was the end of any untoward thoughts about her, and I promised yet again that I was not about to let my friendship with Frank be compromised by any attraction to Thelma; I vowed anew that no matter how much I might want to, I was never going to respond to any of her attempts to seduce me.

Just when I was feeling so good about my newfound determination—cleansed you might say—a finger poked against my shoulder; I turned to see a chest wearing a red and black western shirt standing as close to me as it could get without touching me. I took a step back from the king; my timing was just right to give him enough swinging room to hit me on the side of my head with his fist. I guess I went down, stunned momentarily, 'cause I didn't know what was happening for a minute or two; afterward, when I recovered from my stupor and looked around, the king lay sprawled on the floor under a table, his shiny lizard boots pointing toward the ceiling. A couple of his friends lay on the floor near him holding their hands against their bloodied faces; a guy was hanging on Frank's back trying to pull him away from another member of their posse. By the time I was on my feet and ready to help Frank, he had already thrown one guy halfway across the dance floor and punched the other one back into the chair from which he had attempted to rise.

I grabbed Frank around the waist from behind and began to talk to him as calmly as I could. Thelma took the same stance in front of her husband. Between the two of us, we managed to subdue him.

"Come on, Frank, calm down," I said, "I'm not hurt. He didn't hurt me."

"The hell you say … the goddamn sons a bitch—sucker punching motherfucker." Then, looking down at the addled king, who by then was sitting upright with his head barely protruding from under the table, he added, "Come on, you little bastard. I'll kick your ass again if you fuck with my wife or my buddy; understand, motherfucker?"

The king didn't move, but he nodded affirmatively that he had gotten Frank's message.

"Come on, Frank," I said, "I think the bartender has already called the cops. We need to get out of here."

"I don't give a fuck about the cops. I don't give a fuck about anybody. I'm gonna whip some ass if these drugstore cowboys fuck with me or anybody that even thinks he might know me."

"Come on," I said again, hanging onto his big right arm, "let's go."

By the time we made it to Frank's SUV, we could hear the sirens wailing and getting louder. Frank pulled out of the parking lot and headed up the road back toward town. We might have driven four or five miles before lights began flashing all over hell through the rear window."

"Son of a bitch," I said. "I should have driven." I was clearheaded, but I knew Frank wasn't about to pass a sobriety test.

Frank pulled off the road, rolled his window down, and waited. One police car pulled around and parked in front of the SUV. A second cruiser stopped behind us with its blue lights still flashing.

"Where you goin' in such a hurry?" the deputy asked, peering at Frank as he shined a light into the SUV and looked all three of us over.

"Home," Frank said, "but I wasn't speeding."

"Been drinking?"

"Yeah, a little," Frank responded.

"How little?"

"Maybe five or six beers," Frank said. He probably wasn't lying—it was more than likely he just never kept count.

"Bartender back at the High Country said you tore up his place, beat up some of his customers."

"He lied," Frank said.

"Those guys jumped me," I said from the seat behind Frank, "and Frank defended me." The cop shined his light in my face for a moment to look me over. I guess he decided I didn't matter, so he went back to talking to Frank.

"Bartender says you started it," the deputy said, looking up at Frank, who was still sitting behind the wheel. By then, three other deputies were standing around the car on the driver's side.

"I don't start 'em, I just finish 'em," Frank said through his beer. His beer wasn't bragging; it was just relating the facts. I could truthfully attest to that.

"I want you to get out here where I can look at you," the deputy said.

The officers stepped back from the car as Frank descended from his SUV and stood towering above them. The cop who had been doing the talking asked him for his driver's license. Frank took his wallet out of his pocket and removed his license, which he handed to the deputy. The officer shined a light onto the card, examining it front and back. He walked away from the car momentarily, spoke quietly with one of the other deputies, and then returned to his position in front of Frank.

During the whole process, Thelma hadn't said one word. I felt her hand on my arm that rested on the back of the driver's seat. I looked at her; tears were welling up in her eyes, but she smiled prettily, I suppose trying to give the impression that there was nothing to be concerned about.

"I want you to get on that line in the middle of the road and walk straight down it, one foot in front of the other, for twenty feet," the deputy said.

"Fuck you," Frank said. "I ain't drunk, and I ain't walking down the middle of no goddamn highway."

"Hey, Frank," I said through the open window, "do what they tell you."

"You shut up and stay in the car," the cop said, looking quickly in my direction, then back up at Frank.

"Are you going to walk on that line for me?"

"Fuck you," Frank said.

Almost immediately, the four cops grabbed Frank's arms, turned him around, and pinned him against the SUV. I was surprised that Frank didn't resist their efforts to subdue him. Instead, he placed his hands behind his back and allowed the officers to place handcuffs on his wrists. He walked willingly to the police car and lowered his head to get into the backseat. Frank looked in our direction and yelled something about me driving Thelma home just before one of the cops slammed the door shut.

The arresting officer came to the SUV and told me to get out. He checked me and my driver's license at the same time, and then asked me if I was in any shape to drive. I had not drunk more than a half-dozen beers all night, I told him. Even if I had been stone drunk, the events of the past half hour would have sobered me completely.

"What about Frank?" I asked. "Can we come down now and bail him out?"

"Not for twelve hours," the deputy said. "Come down to the courthouse tomorrow morning after ten o'clock; maybe you can get him out then. Better see a bail bondsman though, 'cause he'll have to post at least a thousand-dollar bond." With that all four policemen got into their cars, spun their vehicles around on the highway, and headed back in the direction from which they came. That left Thelma and me sitting along the highway in the SUV in near total darkness, neither of us speaking.

After a few moments, I turned the key in the ignition; the lights in the dash came on, and the car started up. "Goddamn," I said, looking straight ahead. "What a fucking mess!"

"It's my fault," Thelma said. "He's such a good guy, and I keep fucking him up."

I turned my face slightly in her direction; her eyes were filled with tears, but she wasn't crying. "Not your fault; you didn't do anything wrong," I said. "Not your fault." I patted her arm that rested on the console between us. "Guess I better get you home. Can you drop me off?"

"I can't drive, Lenny. I'm too nervous," she said. "You can have the SUV after you get me home."

I pulled onto the highway. After a few moments, Thelma began to talk. "You know that guy Jerry?"

"What guy?"

"The guy in the red shirt. The one that hit you. You know him?"

"Hell, no."

"I do."

"Where from?"

"My ex-husband," she said.

"Fuck! No wonder Frank was pissed."

"I know," she said. "That's why it was my fault. I shouldn't have danced with him."

"Well, why did you?"

"I don't really know," she said, leaning forward in the seat so she could turn to look me right in the face. "Honestly, I don't really know, 'cause I don't like him much—Frank ought to know that. But he is a good dancer."

"Obviously Frank doesn't like him at all," I said.

"Oh, he doesn't mind him," she said. "He would have been pissed at anyone who danced with me so much." She stopped talking and looked out the window on the other side of the car, "'cept you," she said. "Frank wouldn't mind if I danced with you. I don't think he would mind anything I ever did with you."

"There are some things he would mind," I assured her.

"I don't think so." She smiled suggestively.

"Like I said, there are some things he would mind."

"I don't think so," she said. "Not even what you have on your mind."

"I don't have anything on my mind except getting you home," I said.

"Yeah, I know," she conceded.

We drove on in silence for several more minutes. The conversation had turned in a direction I had not intended, and I didn't know what to say next that would not reveal the confusion I was feeling. Frank's words to me while sitting at the table in High Country flashed through my mind, and suddenly I felt guilty as hell just being in the car alone with his wife. I pushed harder on the accelerator and kept my line of vision trained on the road. I was determined to get her home and away from me as quickly as I could.

"You're going to get a ticket," Thelma said. "You in a hurry?"

"Yes, I am in a hurry," I said with renewed resolve, speaking without looking at her. "I'm going to drop you off then go home and get some sleep. I gotta get Frank bailed out in the morning."

"Oh, OK, if you want to get rid of me … If that's what you really want to do."

"That's not necessarily what I want to do," I said, assuring her that her overture had not gone unnoticed.

"I was just teasing, you know."

"Yeah, I know," I said to her. To myself I added, "Yeah, I know how much you were teasing."

After a half hour of driving, I pulled into the driveway, stopped the engine, and waited for her to get out of the car. She reached for her purse on the floorboard, and then opened the door. The interior lights came on. In the pale glow from overhead, her eyes glistened with the tears she had held back all night. She began to weep.

"Don't cry," I said, looking at her long auburn hair as she opened the door on the passenger side and slid slowly to the ground. "Everything will be alright." My placation didn't seem to help; she was sobbing audibly as she closed the car door.

I had intended to stay in the SUV and make certain Thelma was safely inside the house before I left, but instead I stepped down onto the driveway and waited for her to walk around from the other side of the car. She came to me and stood for a moment with her head resting against my chest, quietly crying, I suppose, for Frank as well as for herself. I put my arm around her consolingly as we walked up the steps. At the door, she inserted the key in the lock, entered the foyer, and immediately turned on a light. "Come on in for a few minutes," she invited.

"I can't," I said. "I can't"

"Just for a minute or two till I feel a little better."

"You and I both know that wouldn't be too smart," I said.

"Don't worry. I won't try to put the make on you, Lenny," she said, smiling through her tears. "I just need someone to talk to for a little while till I pull myself together. I'll make some coffee. Come on," she reached for my hand, "it's alright."

I should have turned and run like hell down the steps back to the car; I realized that, but I didn't do it. I didn't, because that was not what I really wanted to do. Vague thoughts of Thelma's soft breasts against my chest while we were dancing, her moist, warm breathing on my neck, and the shiver in her body as I held her tightly around the waist kept me standing at her door longer than I should have. But I knew I would have to face my best friend in the morning, and I told myself that as much as I might want Thelma, there was no way I would betray Frank, no way I could break the trust he had in me. I pulled my hand away from hers.

She reached for my hand again, looked up through half-closed eyes still wet from crying, and tugged gently at my fingers. "C'mon, Lenny."

"You think it would be OK with Frank?" I asked.

"Course it would," she said. "What's the harm?"

"Guess we can have one cup of coffee before I go. Nothing wrong with that, huh?"

"Course not," she said.

I stepped across the threshold; by then it was three o'clock in the morning. "OK, I'll come in, but just for a few minutes. I can't stay long, 'cause I gotta go bail Frank out of jail at ten," I said as I closed the door behind me.

A Lady I Met at Closing Time

It was almost two in the morning, and Club Lucky, on the west bank of New Orleans, was beginning to empty out. Only four people were still at the bar, and all the customers who had been seated at tables had long ago gone home. Lou, a husky longshoreman, was on his favorite stool at the end of the bar. As usual, he would probably be the last person to leave, and even then, Vince would have to tell him it was time to go home. Hell, Lou never paid any attention to last call. Al had closed down the hamburger joint in the back and had taken a stool next to me. He sat sipping on a beer and wisecracking as usual. Al was a funny guy; he nearly always made me laugh, but not this night; all I wanted was to be left alone.

Seated about three bar stools down was an attractive blonde about thirty-five or so, nicely dressed, and intoxicated; she glanced my way occasionally. I vaguely recalled having seen her in the Club once or twice before, but I hadn't paid much attention to her previously. She could see that Al wasn't exactly tickling my funny bone, and for some reason she got the idea he was picking on me.

"Let the boy alone," she said. "Can't you see he's in no mood for your bullshit?"

Al mussed my hair with one of his big hands (the one without the beer in it) and laughed. "I just don't want him feeling sorry for hisself. He ain't the first one to lose a girl; I know a thing or two about that myself."

"Yeah," she said, "we all got stories to tell, including me, but I don't want you telling them in front of God and everybody else; I guess the boy feels the same way."

I listened, smiling while Al and the lady bantered back and forth. At about five minutes before two, Vince began collecting bottles and unattended glasses from the bar. All of us survivors of the evening filled our glasses one last time and clutched them with both hands while Vince wiped the bar around our elbows. The lady got off her bar stool and moved alongside me, on the side away from Al. Standing with her back to the bar, her face only inches from mine, she spoke just above a whisper. "I don't want to go home tonight."

"You don't?" I teased, keeping my voice low so no one else could hear.

"No, I don't."

"Well, where do you want to go?"

"With you."

"You don't know me."

"You just think I don't," the lady said. "I know all about you."

"What do you know about me?" I asked curiously, thinking that perhaps she had heard rumors about me or knew an acquaintance of mine.

"I know all about you and almost every other man in the world," she said, "and I know how to keep you from feeling sorry for yourself."

"And what can I do for you in return?"

"The same thing."

"The same thing?"

"Yeah, you can do the same thing for me—keep me from being lonely—just for tonight."

I looked at her without speaking for several moments, trying to decide if I wanted to get involved with her.

"No strings attached; no big questions asked," she continued.

"Yeah," I said, my interest piqued.

"Yeah, whatcha say?" She pushed her body against my leg while she looked at me through half-closed eyes.

Vince flashed the lights over the mirror behind the bar, indicating it was time to close. "Time to go home, Lou," he said.

I heard Al and Lou get off their stools, but I never looked in their direction. Al slapped me on the back as he turned to leave. "See ya, kid."

I pawed the air with one hand, acknowledging that he was leaving, without taking my eyes off the blonde, who was almost straddling my leg by then.

"What do you need with me?" I asked her, knowing that we obviously had little in common.

"The same thing you need with me," she said as she kissed the side of my face.

I slid off my bar stool and asked Vince to call a cab. By then, only he, the blonde and I were still in the bar. She had not asked my name, and I had not asked hers.

"You got anything to drink at home?" she asked.

"Bourbon."

"That'll do," she said. "I love bourbon. Bourbon and good loving go together, don'tcha think?"

The ride to my apartment took less than ten minutes. I instructed the cab driver to stop a half block from the house. I helped my companion from the car, and we walked down the cobblestone sidewalk, her high heels clicking and clacking. I just knew we were going to make a clamorous entry and awaken the landlady, the landlady's mother, and her sister at two thirty in the morning. My landlady had already cautioned me about having *loose women* in my apartment; it was against her Catholic beliefs.

"Take your shoes off," I said.

"Why?"

"Because I don't want to wake the landlady."

We stopped. She held onto my arm while she removed one shoe at a time. When we reached the house, I opened the small wooden gate. Through the front yard, up the steps, and through the front door we tiptoed until we reached the door to my apartment. We stopped, and I listened for noise from downstairs that would indicate we had awakened the landlady but heard nothing.

Once inside the apartment, she followed me through the kitchen and into the bedroom. She took a seat with her back against the headboard and her legs stretched out on the bed. "How about a drink?" she asked.

I went into the kitchen and poured straight bourbon for her, then opened a soda water for me. (I had enough bourbon in me already.) As I handed her the drink, she patted the bed with her hand, indicating that I should sit beside her. I kicked off my shoes and sat back alongside her.

"Are you going to tell me who you are?" I asked.

"What difference does it make?" she replied. "Don't you like the way I look, even if you don't know my name?"

"You look great, but I would just like to know something about you."

"Are you going to let me stay even if I don't tell you my name?"

"Sure, you can stay."

"Then let's not discuss me anymore," she said. She sipped from her glass, rolling it around in her hand. "Maybe before the night is out … maybe I'll decide to tell you something about me; meantime, what's bothering you?"

"What do you mean?" I asked, knowing she was referring to Al's comments in the bar.

"You know, your girl troubles; what about that?"

"Nothing much to tell; my girl and I just called it quits, or rather I did, and it's been bothering me."

"And?" she asked, nudging me with her elbow.

"And that's it; she went back to her husband."

"Husband?"

"Yeah, husband."

"Now, this is getting interesting."

"Think so?" I asked.

"Did you want her to go?"

"I don't know."

"Don't know?" she asked, taking a swig from the glass, then handing it to me for a refill as her eyes studied my face.

I went to the kitchen, filled the glass, and returned with the bottle of bourbon, which I set on the table beside the bed.

When I was seated next to her again, she reached for my hand and held it gently against the side of her face. "Tell me about her."

"She's young," I said, "too young to be married, and too young to have all the problems I've caused her."

I thought about the absurd situation in which I found myself, discussing my personal life with someone I knew nothing about. She was an attractive, well-dressed lady, obviously educated. But something was dreadfully wrong in her life that placed her in the bar late that night, with no one she wanted to go home to and no one in particular she wanted to be with. She was with me simply because I was the last man standing at closing time—and she didn't know anything about me; I hadn't even told her my name, and she hadn't asked.

"I'm Dave," I said, thinking it was about time for introductions.

She raised her glass. "Glad to know you, Dave."

"Why me?" I asked.

"What do you mean?"

"Why did you pick me tonight?"

"I didn't pick you," she said. "Fate did, and that's good enough for me. It could have been anybody, but you look like a very nice guy, and fate is seldom wrong."

She took a drink then sighed. "Go on; tell me about your girl; I want to hear."

"She's mixed up, like me," I said, "I think she loves me, but she went back to her husband. California."

"How long?"

"Two weeks now," I said, "and I haven't heard from her."

"Have you tried to get in touch with her?"

"No," I said, "I'm not going to. I don't want to mess up her life any more than I already have."

"Does she know how you still feel about her?"

"I think so."

"But you're not sure?"

"It doesn't matter; I don't want to start that whole thing all over again. I—"

"So, what's really bothering you?" she interrupted, then continued talking, as if a light had suddenly come on in her head. "I'll bet it's your conscience." She smiled as if she knew she had hit upon the truth. Apparently she could see deeper inside me than I could. It was unsettling to think I had met her less than an hour earlier, and she already understood me better than I understood myself; I didn't know anything about her, not even her name.

"Let me take a stab at what is really bothering you, darling," she said. "You know what I think? I think you want to feel noble about it, but instead you feel guilty. What do you think?"

"I don't want to feel noble, and I don't think I have anything to be guilty about."

"Let me ask you a question; and I want you to answer it honestly."

"OK."

"Did you really want her to leave her husband, marry you?"

"Marry? No, not now. Maybe eventually, but not now."

"So you didn't want to get married?"

"Eventually, I would have."

"But weren't you just a little bit relieved when she went back to her husband? Come on now, be truthful."

"I don't think so," I said, "I didn't want to let her go, but I thought it was the best thing for her."

She sat up against the headboard. "Let me hear the whole story so I'll understand; you know, maybe I'm jumping to conclusions without all the facts. Tell me about you and your girl."

"I don't like to talk about it."

"You won't ever get another opportunity like this one," she said. "There is no one better on earth to talk to than me."

"How so?" I asked, managing a whimsical smile.

"I mean there is no one who can understand better than I can. That's what I mean, darling. I don't talk; I don't gossip, and I don't know you or your girlfriend; what's more, I don't want to know. So you can say anything that's on your mind to me, and when I disappear from your life, whatever you tell me disappears with me."

I began to talk about how I met Mary eight months earlier. She was just eighteen and married to a soldier stationed in California. When I met her, they had been married less than a month, and she was saving money to go to California to live with him. Two months after we met, she moved into my apartment. When Joe, her husband, learned about us, he came to our apartment with the family priest. Joe pled with Mary to return to him. When I saw how much he loved her, I realized I could never love her as much.

When I finished talking, the lady sat up on her knees beside me, drank her last drop of bourbon, and began clapping her hands. "Bravo, bravo."

"What's that for?" I asked, surprised at her reaction to my somber story.

"Isn't that what you do for a hero?"

"I don't think I'm a hero," I said. "I just wanted to do the right thing."

She asked, "Do you think Mary loves you?"

"I know she does."

"Then why do you think you did the right thing by letting her go?"

"It was the best thing for her."

"Best for Mary, or maybe best for you?" She toyed with me.

"Maybe both of us."

"Do you really believe that, or is that just convenient for you?"

"Yeah," I said; then I stopped for a moment to think about it. "I believe it." But I was beginning to see that marriage was always out of the question for Mary and me and that I had no choice but to get out of her way, to give her a chance to find happiness with Joe.

"If she is happy with Joe, will it hurt your pride?"

"Of course not," I said incredulously. "Why do you ask that?"

"Because that's the way men are. Every man thinks he is the only one who can make any woman happy. Are you sure you don't feel that way?"

"No, I really do want her to be happy."

"But what if she isn't happy; will you feel guilty?" she asked, and then after a moment said, "You shouldn't, you know. Whether or not you intended it, you may have really saved a marriage that would never have made it if you had not come into her life."

"What do you mean?"

"I know you probably don't want to hear it, and even though I think you are really a nice guy, Joe is better for her than you are. My guess is that Mary didn't understand what a good man he is; maybe she does now."

"Why would you say that?" I asked, a little disappointed that I had not made a better impression on the lady who was sitting on my bed, drinking my bourbon.

"Because he loves her more than he loves himself," she said, "or else he wouldn't have taken her back."

"Are you saying I don't love her?"

"No. Maybe you love her, but not enough, not unselfishly the way Joe does."

"I just wanted her to be happy."

"That's what I meant when I said you were feeling noble about Mary. You want to believe you gave her up so she could be happy. That makes you feel noble, doesn't it? But you really gave her up because it was the easy thing to do."

She reached for the glass on the table beside the bed and motioned for me to fill it again. With a full glass in hand, she continued her analysis.

"If you loved her as much as her husband does, you would have fought for her, and you wouldn't have taken the first opportunity you could find to get out of the relationship."

"How did you become so wise?" I asked, turning to face her.

"I may be wise," she said, swirling the bourbon in her glass, looking away from me, "but I'm not very smart."

"How do you explain that?"

"Well, I know people, and I even know myself, but I don't always do what I should do. That's what I meant about not being very smart;; for example, what am I doing here in bed with someone nearly half my age and me with a husband at home?"

"A husband?" I asked. "Isn't he expecting you home?"

"No," she said. "He knows better. He knew when I left last night that I would spend the night with someone, somewhere."

"Doesn't he care?"

"Very much."

"And doesn't that bother you?"

"Very much."

"Won't he ask about me when you get home?"

"No," she said, "he doesn't want to know anything about you or any other man I might have slept with."

"How about you? Don't you want to know anything about me?"

"Yes, but very little," she said, smiling as she raised her glass in my direction. "Pour me another bourbon, baby."

The lady undressed while I filled the glass. She took a swallow, set the glass down on the table, and then pulled back the covers. "Come on, baby," she said, "I'm going to make you feel better."

I turned out the light, undressed, and got into bed beside her. We embraced. I kissed her face, breasts, and body, unleashing a torrent of emotion in her. Finally, I was learning what she meant when she said she knew everything about me and almost every other man in the world. When it was over, I lay looking up through the darkness, feeling wonderfully exhausted. Shortly, I heard her take a deep breath, and I knew she was sleeping.

Just before seven, the alarm awoke me. The surrealism of the night before came quickly to mind as I saw her lying beside me. I touched her shoulder and nudged her awake.

"Hey, baby, what time is it?" she asked.

"Almost seven."

"Christ, I gotta go," she said, getting quickly out of bed.

I left the room while she dressed. After several minutes she came into the kitchen, where I had poured two cups of coffee.

"Don't mind the way I look," she said.

"You look fine."

"I'll bet you say that to all your women."

"I do." I smiled coyly.

"May I use your phone?"

"Sure," I said, handing it to her and setting a cup of coffee on the table in front of her.

She dialed and waited for someone to answer.

"Louise, let me speak to him." She paused for almost a minute, and then said, "I'm with a friend. I'll be home soon—no, I'll take a cab." She paused and drank some coffee. "Just someone I met last night, no one special ... OK, be there soon. Let me speak with Louise again."

I sat at the table looking at her in disbelief. I suppose I was in awe at the casual and matter-of-fact way she talked to her husband about sleeping with another man. After a moment, she began to speak again, and I assumed Louise was back on the phone.

"How was he last night?"

She listened for a moment then spoke again. "Did he take his medicine?"

She avoided my eyes as she waited for Louise to respond.

"No. I'll be there in about half an hour to help you put him in his chair; yes, I know he needs to lose weight. What else does he have to do but eat? Christ, he can't do anything else!"

She said good-bye to Louise and dialed another number. She requested a taxi and then asked me for my address.

We sat in silence, drinking our coffee while we waited for the cab to come. I tried to make sense out of what I had just heard. Obviously, her husband couldn't walk; obviously too, he knew she was sleeping around but accepted it because he couldn't do anything about it.

"What's wrong with your husband?"

"He's ill," she said without looking at me.

"Did he guess about you and me?"

"More than likely."

"Won't he give you hell when you get home?"

"No. I wish he would sometime; it would make me feel better about myself."

"If I were in his place, I might shoot you."

"Well, he certainly wouldn't do that even if he could."

"Why not?"

"Because he loves me more than he loves himself," she said, holding her coffee cup with both hands at chin level.

"He must be a pretty nice guy."

"He is," she said, "and noble too. But then, how do I explain me?"

"You're nice," I assured her.

"Maybe," she said, "but I damn sure ain't noble."

As we waited in silence, she patted my outstretched hand nervously several times. Slowly tears filled her eyes; then, she quickly smiled and wiped them away.

I walked to the window and watched for the taxicab. When it pulled up, I turned to her. "Aren't you going to tell me your name before you go? I would like to know how to get in touch with you."

"You don't need my name because I won't ever see you again."

"But why?" I asked. "I thought we got along pretty well, didn't we?"

"Yes, maybe too well; you're a nice guy."

"But you don't want to see me again?"

"That's right," she said. "It wouldn't do for either of us."

I watched her as she went down the stairs. She walked out the front door without ever looking back. Just as she closed the door behind her, my landlady appeared in the hall and looked up in my direction. "What was that woman doing upstairs?" she demanded.

"Using the phone," I said, and then I turned and walked back into my apartment.

Doggone

It was Sunday, the final day of the Monterey Peninsula All-Breed Dog Show. I was just driving around with nothing better to do with my time and no place in particular to be, so I stopped by to investigate why so many cars were at the city park and why so many people had gathered there on that pleasant, sunny afternoon. As I got out of my car, I looked around to make certain no one was there who would recognize me and think that attending dog shows was something I did on a regular basis.

The place was a bustle of activity—people hurrying here and there, some holding onto leashes to which were attached at the opposite ends variously sized, coiffured, powdered, and perfumed little animals, which, if examined closely, appeared to be dogs. Roped-off and ribbon-cordoned sections designated the holding areas for different breeds of dogs. In each area, a black and yellow placard balanced atop a long wrought iron stake described the origins and history of that particular breed. Dog owners preened, brushed, and pampered their pets inside the roped-off areas.

The main arena was a large, ovoid ring that encircled nearly a half acre of the park and was bounded by red and white braided nylon ropes. Blue ribbons symbolizing victory graced the chrome-plated steel posts that evenly dotted the perimeter. The officials' area, located at one end of the oval, was tastefully decorated in red, white, and blue. Four chairs, covered in white and reserved for the judges, sat on a dais raised a conspicuous (appropriately dignified) foot above ground level. On the other end of the oval was an obstacle course where dogs were being put through their paces as I made my way closer to the arena. People watching the competition oohed and aahed, and the judges, with clipboards in hand, were making notations (I supposed) of each and every omission or breach of dog etiquette witnessed or imagined.

Outside the arena and near the parking area were variously sized tents, set up as concession stands for the hawking of event programs, tasteful souvenirs, dog-related magazines, leashes, collars, dog sweaters, and formal dog wear. There were refreshment stands selling hot dogs, Greek sandwiches, and almost anything else one might dare eat with a glass of lemonade or another nonalcoholic beverage. In one tent, people could have their own portraits painted or those of their dogs if they were so inclined.

I quickly discerned that I understood much more about the commercial aspects of the activity surrounding the arena than about the particular nuances of the dog judging taking place inside the arena. Plainly and simply, I was there only by coincidence; I had no knowledge whatsoever about the delicate breeding and training I imagined was entailed in qualifying a dog for the events I was witnessing and about to witness. All the dogs I had ever owned had been curs; they were not trained to heel, stay, or fetch; they ate table scraps, slept outside, and farted.

The viewing area wasn't particularly crowded. Plenty of room remained for sitting on the ground with one's legs fully extended. So I took a seat in the grass, stretched out my limbs, and hayseeded a blade of grass between my teeth a la Huckleberry Finn. I sat there for several minutes, craning my neck and turning my head back and forth, watching dogs that looked like greyhounds (only skinnier) lead their owners around the ring at the pace of a first-place finisher at the dog track. I wondered why these particular dogs were taking part in a beauty contest instead of chasing Casey down at the local track.

On one turn of my head, I became aware of a shapely leg positioned just inches from my right ear. I looked five degrees further to the right and saw another leg just as shapely as the first. I was almost afraid to look up at the owner of those legs for fear that I would see right up her skirt. While I was deciding whether or not to look, she crossed her legs and came to a squat, then seated herself right next to me, her skirt brushing my head on the way down. I pretended I didn't see her and went right on looking intently at the greyhounds or whatever breed they were, letting her know right then and there that nothing could distract me from the pleasures of dog watching, which was obviously what I was there for. After the judges had given ribbons to the three or four ugliest dogs in the competition, I allowed myself to notice my new companion and to smile and say hello.

"Hi," she said.

"I'm Jeff Stone," I said, extending my hand. She shook it with the tips of her fingers as if she were afraid she might get dog doo-doo on her.

"Enjoying the show?" I asked.

"Yes," she said, "although, quite frankly, I don't know much about dog shows."

"It's never too late to learn," I said, hoping I had gained enough knowledge about dog shows during the past ten minutes to impress her, "but to tell you the truth, I'm here just because I like dogs." I wasn't certain where that last part about liking dogs came from, and I knew I was traveling down an uncertain road.

She didn't respond, just looked straight ahead at the dogs in the arena.

"Yep, I like some of them better than people," I said to no one in particular but loud enough for her to hear.

"I know what you mean," she said, looking at me cautiously and then quickly turning her head away.

"Well, aren't we the sore ass?" I thought to myself, taking another quick glance at her and deciding that maybe she wasn't as good-looking as I had first thought.

She didn't look back in my direction again during the entire judging of the English spaniel competition. And even though I oohed and aahed and gave out with an occasional "Bravo!" as the Boston terriers paraded by on tiny legs and feet that looked like black fingers daubed in white wash, she didn't give me a glance. When the miniature collies jumped through hoops and walked up ramps and through confusing labyrinths, she failed to clap, though I and the other spectators, who were well aware of proper dog show etiquette, applauded. By then I had taken a third and fourth look at her, each peek longer than the previous, and had decided she was really pretty damn cute. I was hoping she would see how helpful I could be in the instant situation and that she would turn to me for advice and perhaps— although I knew I was probably stretching things— companionship.

Finally I said, "I didn't get your name."

"That's because I didn't give it." Pleased with herself, she smiled without looking directly at me.

"Do you have a dog?" I continued the conversation.

"Yes," she said, now smiling genuinely and looking full faced at me. "Do you?"

"Uh, no; no, I don't," I said, half-surprised that she was talking to me after ignoring me for more than twenty minutes.

"I have a schnauzer," she said proudly. "I just love schnauzers, don't you?"

Schnauzer? Schnauzer? What the hell was a schnauzer? I didn't know a schnauzer from a schnitzel, but I couldn't tell her that. I finally had her talking to me, and I had to find a way to keep her interested in what I had to say.

"I sure do," I heard someone say using my voice. "In fact, I have a schnauzer myself." I was trying my best to drum up a picture in my mind of a schnauzer before she asked me something about them that a schnauzer owner should know.

"I thought you said you didn't have a dog," she said with a smile that told me she didn't believe a thing I was saying.

But I was undaunted. "Well, I meant I don't have him now because someone stole him."

"Stole him?" she asked with alarm, incredulity and genuine concern in her voice. "When?"

I looked all around trying to see a cordoned off area labeled "schnauzers," but no such luck. I inventoried my mental file on dogs and came up with nothing except— oh, yes, then I remembered: a schnauzer would be one of those foot-long hot-dog-looking things with short legs and ears and a tail. Sure, I remembered, and with newfound confidence, I heard the guy with my voice say dejectedly, "About six months ago."

I had put myself in a sad state of mind and was feeling too much grief to say anything more at that moment, so I just waited for her to console me.

"I don't know what I would do if someone stole Gretel," she said.

"I know what you mean," I said, keying in on the German name. "I miss Baron terribly."

"Baron?" she said. "What a cute name for a schnauzer!"

"Yeah, Baron, like Red Baron; he was my companion," I said. "I got him when he was six weeks old, and he had been with me for the past three years. But a few months ago, someone broke into my apartment while I was at work and stole Baron. Of course they stole my television and my computer too, but Baron was the most important thing they took."

By then I almost made myself cry. Baron had become very real to me, and I proceeded to tell her about the long walks Baron and I took together, the way he rode in a basket on my ten-speed bicycle, and of course the way he sat on my lap when I drove the car.

"I left Gretel in a good kennel, so I'm sure she will be fine."

"Oh, I'm sure she will be OK," I assured her. "What's your name again?"

"I'm sorry," she said. "It's Gwendolyn; call me Gwen."

"Good; call me Jeff."

"Jeff," she said, placing her hand on my arm, "you are the first guy I have ever met that owned a schnauzer. But you know what?"

"What?"

"I've concluded not everyone should own a schnauzer; it takes a special kind of person, you know what I mean?"

I nodded that I did, knowing that I was special and a pretty good guy, except for a propensity to lie a little when the occasion called for it.

"You have to have a certain personality and an understanding way to appreciate them," she continued. "Don't you agree?"

I did of course, and I said so. "Oh, yes; I agree," I said, wanting to get Baron back into the conversation. "I would like to have another schnauzer if I can't find Baron, but right now I just can't give up on finding him."

I sat with the palms of my hands on the ground beside me and my chin tilted back slightly. I'm sure I looked very sad, even close to distraught. I felt her hand, small and warm and smooth, touch mine and then squeeze it gently. Then I felt even more sadness—as much as was appropriate for the occasion—and I believe that real tears welled up in my eyes.

"You know," I said, "if those people ever knew just how much sadness they have caused me by taking my little schnauzer, they never would have stolen him."

She squeezed my hand again.

"Baron was the sweetest dog. I wish he had been able to run and play with your Gretel, " I said, " but of course that might not have been possible since Gretel is in— where did you say you are from?"

"Seattle," she said, then sighed sadly, "Seattle."

"Seattle," I said. "Gretel is in Seattle, and Baron is in only God knows where."

She moved closer to me, lifting her hand and mine onto my lap.

"What are you doing in Monterey?" I asked.

"I'm on vacation, on my way to San Diego. I'll be leaving tomorrow morning."

By then I was bold enough to envision a whole evening and a memorable night together—one that she would write explicit details about in her diary, and later, after she was married, she would tear out the revealing pages so her husband would never read about the torrid affair.

I told her about all the places she should go while in Monterey. She had not been on the Seventeen-Mile Drive, seen Carmel Valley, gone to dinner at the Sardine Factory, or had a drink at the Hog's Breath Saloon. Before the brown Labs had finished parading through the arena, she said she wanted to do all those things, and she had agreed to dancing and dinner after the dog show. Further, she had said that perhaps she could delay her departure for San Diego one more day if I might have time to get together the next evening.

"Are you feeling better?" she asked.

"Some," I said. "I'm sorry about being so down, but when you started talking about your schnauzer, all the memories of Baron came back. I really do miss him."

"Well, maybe you will find him yet," she said. "Just don't give up hope." She patted my hand reassuringly.

"I hope so. But let's not talk about it anymore; it just makes me sad."

"I love that in a man," she said, hugging me. "You're not afraid to show your true feelings. Why, how many men would almost cry over a dog?"

Not many, I surmised. I nodded knowingly, hopefully communicating that I was too aggrieved to continue down that train of thought.

After a few moments, she stood and then raised herself upon her toes. "I wonder if there are any schnauzers here at the show," Gwen asked, looking all around us.

"Maybe," I said, standing on my toes also and looking toward the holding areas. Then I saw them. They were probably forty or fifty feet away.

"Over there," I pointed, heading toward the area where I had seen the schnauzers.

She followed behind me, holding my hand as we ran excitedly. When I stopped and pointed at the hot dogs on tiny legs, she looked puzzled. Suddenly she let go of my hand and stepped back away from me. "These aren't Schnauzers!"

"They're not?" I gasped, very surprised.

She said nothing but looked a bullet right through my head.

"What does Gretel look like?" I asked.

"Like a schnauzer," she said. "Obviously, you've been putting me on, making a fool of me—damn you—and I fell for your story." There was no longer a hint of a smile on her face.

"Look, it wasn't a story," I said. "Baron looked more schnauzerly than these dogs."

I checked the black and yellow placard that read: "Dachshund—there are three varieties of dachshund, etc., etc.

"How do you think he looked, then?" she asked knowingly, biting her lower lip.

For a minute, I thought she would cry, and I didn't know how I would handle it if she did. Then I decided I would try a little more of my irresistible humor on her.

"Well, to tell the truth," I said, "I haven't seen Baron or any other schnauzer for so long, I have forgotten how he looked."

I hoped she would smile at that and see a tinge of humor in it, but she didn't. Instead, she turned and walked away from me, stiff-backed.

I yelled after her, "I'm sorry; I didn't mean to mislead you; it's just that I wanted to go out with you." I ran after her, caught up with her, and took her by her elbow. I tried to make her understand, to let her know a little bit at a time that I had made up the story because I wanted so desperately to get to know her and go out with her. How bad could that be?

"Really," I said, "so maybe Baron wasn't a schnauzer; maybe he was one of those little, long dogs; I don't remember; I loved him just the same. So what difference does it make?"

She looked at me in disgust but didn't answer. Instead she walked briskly away from me again.

I ran after her and caught up with her, but she wouldn't stop walking. I turned around to face her and walk backward in front of her as she strolled determinedly toward her car. "OK, so I made the whole thing up," I said, "but I did it to get your attention, to get to know you."

She pushed me aside, causing me to stumble and fall on my rear end. I looked over my shoulder to see her striding down the row of cars where she apparently had parked her own vehicle. I dusted off the seat of my pants and ran after her again.

"We had a pretty good thing going. Why spoil it now?"

She stopped, turned toward me, and waited for me to catch up with her. I knew then that I had persuaded her of my good intentions. I thought for certain she, as a reasonable woman, would conclude I wasn't a bad guy after all and that while my approach may have had its flaws, it was somewhat ingenious; I hoped she might still enjoy spending the evening—if not the night—with me. I put my hand on her arm and smiled, looking into blue eyes that reminded me of Seattle's summer skies. She smiled back as I congratulated myself for my persistence and my unquestionable charm.

Her smile broadened. "Fuck off, buster," she said.

She turned and walked briskly to her car.

With my hands in my pockets, I stood watching as she revved the engine, sped between two rows of parked cars, and then zoomed out of the show area. The white Mazda with the Washington state license plate quickly disappeared from sight.

"I'll be doggone," I said.

Finishin' Touches

It was the fourth time in less than a week she had called me after midnight! I had already sworn that no matter what happened, I wouldn't go down there again—even if Leon beat the hell out of her. How many times did I have to tell her to get herself and her two kids out of that damn situation? But there I was putting on my trousers to go referee another fight between my daughter and her live-in boyfriend.

"Daddy," she said through her sobs, "Leon is beating me up again."

"I ain't doin' a damn thing but defendin' myself from you, you crazy bitch," I heard Leon, my common-law son-in-law, yell from somewhere in their three-room trailer.

"Julie," I said, "what's going on?"

"Melvin," Leon yelled at the phone for my benefit, "tell this crazy daughter of yours to let me alone."

"Daddy, he hit me again," Julie sobbed.

"You lyin' bitch," I heard Leon shout; this time his voice faded away, and I heard a door slam and the phone drop against the floor.

"Where are you going?" I could hear Julie scream, probably projecting her voice out the door toward the broken down 1982 Chevrolet Malibu that Leon drove back and forth to work whenever it would start. The remainder of the time, he hitched a ride if he was lucky enough to catch one. Otherwise, he walked wherever he might be going to do his handyman jobs. Most of the time, he just didn't bother working.

Julie, nearly thirty-two, was my second daughter. She met Leon somewhere in California when she was rebounding from the breakup of her fourth, fifth, or sixth "this time it is the real thing" relationship. Her mother and I had given up hope she would ever get married; her schizophrenia had always gotten in the way. But somehow she and Leon managed to stay together for better or worse. Nearly two years after they first met, Julie got pregnant. As it turned out, her relationship with Leon was as turbulent as all the others, with the added strain of a grandchild to worry about. We sent Julie money to come home, so we could get her some professional help. When she arrived, Leon was with her. By then the boy was already a year old, and Julie was pregnant with her baby girl.

Knowing Julie's unstable tendencies, I was inclined to occasionally give Leon the benefit of the doubt. On the surface, he was not a bad guy—laid-back, unambitious, and likable enough. He was a sign painter and a damn good one, but he fancied himself an artist too good to do work that might callus his hands. Thus, most available work was usually below a man of his talents.

"I'm coming. I'm on my way now," I told Julie, but I knew she was no longer on the phone to hear me. I stopped at the bathroom mirror long enough to run a comb through my hair and to dab some cold water on my eyes before heading out to the garage. Their trailer was about five miles outside of town. It would take me fifteen minutes to get there.

I knocked, rested my head on my arm against the door casing, waiting and dreading the ordeal ahead of me. "Did he hit you?" I asked Julie when she opened the door.

"No, but he was threatening to when I called you." I could see that Julie had overreacted in order to get me involved in another one of their domestic squabbles.

"I sure as hell wanted to," Leon said, "but I didn't."

"He didn't work again today," Julie said, "just laid around on his lazy ass. The kids don't have milk. He doesn't care; he's a bum, Dad." She turned on the coffeepot. "Want some coffee?"

"No, honey. Food stamps all gone?"

"They were used up two days ago."

"How about the money I gave you?"

"I put gas in Leon's car and bought cigarettes."

"Christ, I can see you two have your priorities straight," I said.

I pulled out a chair and sat down at the kitchen table. Leon and Julie seated themselves at the head and foot and lit up cigarettes.

Leon began talking. "I tried to go to work, but—"

"What stopped you?" Julie raised her voice sarcastically, blowing smoke in the general direction of Leon's face.

"You did," Leon replied with the same intensity.

"Any excuse to lay on your ass." She stabbed the cigarette out in an ashtray, pushed her chair back from the table, and crossed her arms.

"OK!" I interrupted. "Your neighbors have heard enough this week. It's nearly one thirty in the morning, and I'm damn tired of driving over here. Something has to change."

"He won't change," she said pitifully, tears filling the corners of her eyes. She wiped at them with her open hand.

"It ain't my fault, Mel. She's so goddamn jealous, calls everywhere I work accusin' the office girls of screwin' me. She won't let me work."

"Julie, why do you do that kind of stuff?" I said, exasperated. I had had the same discussion about her insane jealousy at least half a dozen times in the past six months.

"Dad, he has an offer to work full time painting cars at a detailing shop, but he won't go."

"Why, Leon?" I asked in disbelief.

"'Cause that's not what I want to do," Leon said, as if he had a pocket full of hundred-dollar bills and all the options in the world.

"Goddamn, man, don't you think you need to work somewhere even if it isn't what you want to do?" I said, exasperated.

"Not when I can make a livin' doin' what I want," he said. "I got a big job goin' right now, a huge sign down at Libby Chevrolet. All it needs is the finishin' touches—fifteen hundred bucks."

"Why didn't you go finish it today?" I asked. I had heard Leon brag before about all the money he could make doing sign painting, but I had never seen much evidence of it. At least every other month, I provided Julie money to pay the rent on the trailer or to pay the electrical bill that kept the power company from discontinuing service.

"She didn't want me to leave the house," he said. " She started screamin' 'bout me makin' out with the office girls. I went down there yesterday to work on the sign again, but she called thirty minutes after I got there accusin' me of fuckin' one of the office girls, so I came home."

"Julie," I said, "Did you do that again?"

"Dad, but I know he's lying; he's got something going on with one of the girls, Wilma or something like that."

"Jesus Christ, Julie, who in the hell would want him besides you?" I said before I could consider my words. "Sorry, Leon. Sorry, but you people gotta do something for the sake of the kids. If you can't get along, you need to go your separate ways."

"That's just what he wants." Julie began to cry frantically. "He wants to get away from me and the children. He doesn't care."

"Suits me," Leon said. "Suits me fine; I'm sick of this shit."

"You bastard!" Julie raised her voice again. "Sorry bastard. Go ahead. Go find Wilma down at Libby's. Finishing touches, my ass! I know where you want to put the finishing touches, and it isn't on any sign you're painting for Mr. Libby— it's on his goddamn secretary."

"Damn!" I said. "Damn! I've had enough. I'm washing my hands of both of you if you don't use some common sense."

"I'm sorry," Julie said. "I don't want to cause you problems, Dad."

"Me neither," Leon said.

"Well what are you going to do about it?" I asked for what seemed like the hundredth time in a week.

"We're going to get some professional counseling," Julie said, "for the sake of the kids."

Leon nodded his head in agreement, but I doubted that anything had been accomplished by rehashing the same old issues or making the same hackneyed promises. I was surprised when, after a few moments, he got up from his chair and walked around the table to where Julie was seated. He bent and kissed her on the side of the face. "I love you, honey," he said.

"I love you too," Julie replied, putting one arm around his neck and returning the kiss.

"Damn," I said, standing up. "You two people are impossible. I am tired of your same old answers. Do you think kissing each other is going to fix this mess? I am not walking out of here tonight without getting something resolved. We've got real problems here. What about those two kids?" I pointed toward the closed bedroom door. I assumed the four-year-old boy and the two-year-old girl had learned to sleep through hell and high water, or else they were hiding under their covers. "What about them?"

"Why are you angry, Daddy?" Julie began to cry. "Don't you want us to try?"

"No," I said, "I am tired of your trying. I don't want you to try; I want you to succeed!"

"What do you want us to do?" Julie asked.

"I want Leon out of the trailer, and I want you to get some real help."

"I don't want him to go, Daddy," she said. "I love him."

"OK," I said, "then you two can fend for yourselves; I'm through. In the morning, I am calling Child Protection.

"Please, Daddy, don't do that. We'll get some help, I promise. I will call family counseling tomorrow, and we'll get started." She looked at Leon. "We'll do it tomorrow, won't we, honey?"

Leon nodded affirmatively.

"You two have worn me out, Julie," I said. "I'm going home. I'll ask Mother to come over in the morning to help you. Maybe she has more patience than I do."

"Thank you, Daddy."

Julie gratefully wrapped her arms around me and lay her head on my shoulder. I held her for a few moments. I was preparing myself for more phone calls in the middle of the night and more trips to the trailer, swearing each one was my last.

Leon stood silently watching Julie and me. His eyes met mine, and I saw in them a resolve I had not seen before. I wondered how many more days would pass before Julie called me to let me know he hadn't come home from work. I realized that his leaving would break her heart and that she and the children would need my wife and me more than ever. I couldn't predict how things might turn out, but at least I knew they were about to change.

"What are you going to do tomorrow, Leon?" I asked.

"I've got to go down to Libby Chevrolet and put the finishin' touches on that sign I've started."

The Vigil

She watched him from her chair next to the bed; his breathing was labored now, his eyes closed. Although the doctor had not said so, she knew that death could come at any moment. She got up from the chair and steadied herself against the bed as she gently wiped the perspiration from his brow.

"There, darling," she said. "It won't be long now".

She knew her weeks-long vigil was coming to an end. During all the days and nights she had been at his bedside, he had not spoken. The stroke had silenced him three months ago, and she expected that he would breathe his last breath without ever regaining consciousness. She prayed that he was not in pain and that his journey to the forever would be painless and peaceful. She bent to kiss his furrowed brow.

"I love you, James," she said. Then she thought about all the times she had not said those words to him when she should have. Even when he had told her that he loved her, she had found it hard to frame her thoughts in those words and tell him she loved him too. Now, when he could no longer hear or see or know that she was in the room, the words came easily to her.

She sat down in the chair, turned on the reading lamp, and opened her Bible to the Song of Solomon. Her eyes were drawn to the words "Many waters cannot quench love, neither can the floods drown it."

"Nor can fire destroy it," she said aloud, "nor can trial by fire."

"Rebecca."

She thought she heard him whisper from the bed. She stood and leaned her face over his and only a few inches away. "Yes, darling," she said. "What is it?" But he said nothing.

She sat down again without taking her eyes off his face. She watched carefully to see if his lips moved to speak her name. After several moments, her eyelids grew heavy, and she dozed. She thought she was awakened by the soft whisper of her name once again, but she couldn't be sure. Then she realized it was her name she had heard, but it came from a different place and a long-ago time.

"Rebecca … Rebecca," his young voice beckoned to her from out of the darkness. Now she could see herself as she was at sixteen. She was sleeping beside Gloria, Jim's sister, and Jim was calling her name from the doorway. "Rebecca … Rebecca."

She slipped on her robe and crossed the room to fall into his arms. She placed her hand over his mouth to keep him from speaking. "You'll wake up everybody," she whispered. "You may have already awakened Gloria. Now be quiet."

They stood outside the door, holding each other and kissing passionately. Jim was home on Christmas leave from the Navy, and Rebecca was spending the night with Gloria, her best friend. She loved Gloria but sometimes felt as if she was exploiting her in order to be with her pal's brother. She knew her mother would never have allowed her to spend the night in Jim's home if Rebecca and Gloria were not such good friends. Such a situation would be tantamount to "just asking for trouble," her mother would have said.

Rebecca pushed him away to allow herself to catch her breath. "Why are you calling me in the middle of the night?" she teased.

"Because I want to make love to you."

"When are you going to marry me?" she quipped, pushing her finger against his chest.

"As soon as you are eighteen." He kissed her again before allowing her to push him away and slip back into Gloria's room.

* * *

"Rebecca?" It was his voice on the phone.

"James? Where are you?"

"Ten blocks away. I want to see you."

"I can't do that."

"Why not? Don't you want to?"

"Yes, I want to. I have missed you."

"Meet me someplace, just for a little while … for the old times," he said.

She had been inside a motel room only once before, and that was on her honeymoon nearly ten years earlier. Now she was alone in a room with James, whom she had not seen in more than a dozen years. They spent the afternoon together, rekindling old fires that should have burned out long ago. When the day was over, she wondered if she could say good-bye to him, but she knew she had no choice.

"I can't do this again," she said.

"Why not?" he asked with disappointment in his voice.

"Because I can't do this to my husband."

"You love me, don't you?"

"I wouldn't have done what I did today if I didn't love you." That would be as close as she would come to telling him how much she really loved him. It scared her to think about it.

As she combed her hair and applied her makeup, she thought about what she would say to her husband. He was a good man, and he did not deserve an unfaithful wife. She looked at herself in the mirror and began to cry.

Jim placed his hands on her shoulders. He turned her so that she was facing him. "I'm sorry," he said. "I didn't mean to cause you pain. I just had to see you."

"We can't do this again," she said. "Promise me."

"I promise," he said. "I won't ever ask you again … but if you want to see me, let me know, and I will be here."

He held her close to him, gently stroking her hair. "The last thing I would ever want to do would be to hurt you," he said. "I won't call you, and I won't try to see you, but I will love you always."

She wanted to tell him she loved him, but she did not wish to be guilty of more betrayal against her husband and family. She stood quietly in his arms with her head on his shoulder.

"I want you to know," he said, "that no matter where I go or what I do, I will always love you. I'll love you until the day I die."

She held him tighter, knowing that he truly loved her, that he had never gotten over her.

He continued," And when I die, my last conscious thought will be of you."

Twenty years went by; she had not heard from him during all that time. Six months after her husband died, she received a phone call from Jim asking if she needed anything. He had divorced his wife a year earlier and was living alone. Half a year later, James and Rebecca married. They planned to make up for all the time lost in the past four decades, but Jim's stroke came only five years after their wedding.

* * *

"Rebecca." She was sure she heard the whisper again.

She stood by the bed and listened more closely. As she bent to kiss his parched lips, she saw them move and heard her name pronounced barely audibly: "Rebecca."

She embraced him as she laid her head on his chest. "Yes, James, I'm here; I'm with you," she said.

She raised her head and looked into his face, watching for his lips to form her name, knowing they would never move again.

Getting Even with Granny

S he looked very surprised, but she couldn't have been any more surprised than I was that I had actually said what I had just said.

"Do you ever fart, Granny?"

It wasn't as if the words had simply slipped out of my mouth; I couldn't claim that excuse. There was no doubt that what I had said was spoken with malice aforethought. As a matter of fact, I had deliberated my words for several minutes before actually saying them. It was just that I couldn't have stood the situation much longer, and I would never have forgiven myself for missing an opportunity to finally get even with my maternal grandmother (whom I loved very much) one time. If I had failed to say the words that had been playing devilishly at the edge of my consciousness for several days, the opportunity would probably have been lost forever. So after a few seconds of waiting for her response, I pressed her for an answer. "Well, do you?"

Granny quickly looked around the room for help from someone, my dad or my mom. Then she leaned her head in the direction of the kitchen to see if anyone was there who would come to her rescue, perhaps condemn me for my outrageous, impertinent behavior and put a halt to my attempts to push the issue further. But I had been careful to note that Granny and I were alone before I ever spoke those nefarious few words. My mother had excused herself and gone upstairs a few minutes before the devilish scene transpired; my dad had not come home from work yet. It was just me and my seventy-eight-year-old granny alone in the family den. Seeing the situation for what it was, she began her own defense.

"Don't talk to me that way," she said, half-pouting.

"You can tell me," I teased, smiling at her. "I won't tell anyone."

Granny pursed her lips in and out several times, as if she was about to speak. Instead, she folded her wrinkled arms together across her chest and leaned back in the rocker with her eyes closed. She heaved a sigh of disgust and rocked slowly back and forth. She sat that way for what seemed like a very long time, not speaking, not even opening her eyes to watch the Lawrence Welk rerun playing on the television in front of us, which in itself was enough to convince me just how upset I had made my poor grandmother. After several minutes, she opened her eyes and looked in my direction through the brownest, beadiest little eyes you would ever hope to see. "Psshhhee," she said, sounding as if she was leaking air. She closed her eyes one more time in total frustration and heaved another long sigh, designed, I knew very well, to elicit an apology, which I reluctantly made to her with the best feigned sincerity I could muster.

"I'm sorry, Granny; I didn't mean to upset you."

"I'm sorry too," she said, "but I cannot accept your apology."

"You sure, Granny?"

"Are you really sorry?"

"Didn't I say I was sorry, Granny?" I said. "I really mean it; I should never have said it."

Damn! Damn! Damn! I could have kicked myself for giving in so easily when I clearly had her on the ropes, ready for the knockout punch. But I realized that an apology was essential to my survival, because I was treading on dangerous ground. My grandmother had a way of making my character flaws take on momentous dimensions when relating events to my father, so my apology was a pure precaution.

"OK, then, I accept," she said, smiling at me.

If my granny was anything, she was forgiving, and she relished giving out pardons, especially to someone completely undeserving like me. She smiled, uncrossed her arms, and moved back into her rocker. "And a one, and a two, and a—" Lawrence waved the baton toward the orchestra as Granny swayed and smiled, convinced that she had prevailed in our little skirmish and probably feeling sanctimonious for having accepted my apology. She could just as easily have chosen retribution by squealing to my father about my bad manners and poor taste, or worst yet, by telling my mother what I had done. My mother, of course, would have blown the whole thing way out of proportion when she told my dad. With that realization, I got up from my chair, walked the six feet to my granny's rocker, and bent over to gratefully kiss her on the forehead. She had won, and I could tell she knew it.

My problems with my grandmother had begun no more than two days after she had arrived for her annual three-month visit. It took no longer than those two days for her to take over the controls for the big television set in the family den, which meant that I was relegated to watching my favorite shows on the fifteen-inch version sitting on top of the bureau in my bedroom. Once in a while, I managed to get the control for the big TV and turn on The Simpsons or MTV or some other "inane" program that, according to Granny, ".he shouldn't be allowed to watch." And of course, when Mother or Dad were in the room, they would side with my mom's mom, and one or the other would suggest that I "let Granny watch her programs," which included the above mentioned Lawrence Welk, The Partridge Family, Little House on the Prairie, and almost everything on Nick At Nite.

Now, I have nothing against Nick At Night; in fact, I watch many of the same programs my grandmother likes to watch, but as far as I'm concerned, there is more to see on television, and we will never experience anything new if we continually live in the past. We need to venture beyond our own experiences, even to the point of watching something as radical as BET or the Entertainment Channel or, God forbid, MTV. But Granny didn't agree with that.

"Trash, trash, trash," she would say loud enough for my mother and father to hear every time I turned on any of those shows in her presence.

"Let Granny watch her programs," my dad would say without looking up from his newspaper. Tranquility was his aim—peace at any price. Me? My aim would soon be vengeance on my dear old grandmother.

It was easy to see that Granny had been a pretty woman when she was younger, and she was still very attractive for her age. She and my grandfather had lived quite comfortable lives. Grandpa had doted on her, and she had grown accustomed to having her way. Since his death about three years earlier, she had not wanted to live alone, so she spent rotating three-month intervals with each of her four children. The summers were our turn, because we lived in Michigan while the rest of mother's family lived in Florida, where it was too hot for Granny in July, August, and September.

My grandmother was not a selfish woman at all. In fact, she was very genteel and thoughtful, but for some reason she considered it her duty to protect me from all the wickedness of the modern world. She did not accept the changing moralities she continually witnessed on television. And she apparently saw it as her duty to keep me from being exposed to such distasteful things.

"What's this world coming to next?" she exclaimed one evening when I inadvertently tuned to The Jerry Springer Show. "You shouldn't be watching that," she continued loudly enough to make my mother scream from the kitchen in response, "Are you watching that filth again?"

"No, mother, I'm not," I said loudly, with obvious irritation in my voice.

"He is too," my grandmother said, looking at me and wrinkling her jaw to give the appearance of an elongated dimple. "You shouldn't lie to your mother," she continued, eying me up and down.

I handed the TV control to my grandmother, walked briskly to the back patio, and sat down with my arms folded across my chest. I was seething. After a few moments, I heard Lawrence Welk coming from the den, and I knew that Granny would be rocking back and forth, smiling contentedly. It was right then and there that I made up my mind to get even with her.

A few nights later, when I was walking past my grandmother's bedroom door, I heard her saying her prayer. "And dear Lord, bless Jim and Angela, and Lord bless little Jimmy and lead him unto a righteous path, because only you, Lord, know where he's headed if he keeps going like he is."

I listened for a moment longer, knowing that I shouldn't be standing by Granny's door. I was puzzled why she thought she had to pray for me to change my ways, when in fact, I believed I was a pretty thoughtful and well- behaved kid. I was always courteous to my teachers and elders and helpful to my mother, and I made good grades. I didn't curse much, and I never drank beer like a lot of the other guys my age.

"Damn," I said, almost regretting it immediately. "She should really be subjected to bad behavior." So I thought maybe there was some way I could hassle her a little. I just wanted to get even—to make her think twice and be grateful for my numerous good qualities, but I didn't have any idea how to do it.

Just as I turned to walk to my room, I heard the loudest farumph, followed by a second farumph not quite as loud as the first. At first I was puzzled. Then, I realized, incredulously, that Granny was farting. It was then and there that I devised my plan to call it to her attention the very next time she embarrassed me or said something to wrest away control of the television.

Anyway, that's why I said what I did.

"Granny, do you ever fart?" Just to think about it made me laugh. And I really believed I would feel some kind of victory, some vindication, when I said it. Instead, there I was, apologetically kissing my granny on the forehead and her sitting there in her rocker lapping it up like a kitten with its milk.

Defeated, I sat down and settled back on the couch to keep Granny company until the Lawrence Welk show finished.

Suddenly, Granny sprang from her chair and walked hurriedly toward the stairs. Just as she mounted the first step and raised her foot toward the second one, a loud farumph erupted from somewhere under her long black dress.

"Excuse me," she said demurely, looking back over her shoulder at me. "Must have been the prunes I ate."

Without ever acknowledging that I had heard anything at all, I quickly changed the TV to the MTV channel and turned up the volume as loud as it would go.

After a few moments, Mother walked into the den with her hands on her hips.

"Just what do you think you are doing?"

"Nothing," I said.

"Well, let Granny watch her programs!"

"I was," I said, "but for some reason she wanted to watch MTV this evening."

A Road Not Taken

I often wonder if anyone's life turns out the way they planned or expected.

Looking back honestly at a time when we were young, most of us will conclude we had little control over the kinds of people we would eventually become. Our lives just happened, and without our knowledge, we suddenly were someone we never intended to be. Was it predestined, or could we have changed the outcome? Would our lives be better today if the choices made at the many junctures of our lives had been different, or would they have turned out the same regardless of the unfortunate choices made or the roads traveled to get here?

About four years ago, my sister, Marge, called to tell me that Janie Taggard and her husband of thirteen years were divorcing. I had just begun coping with the discovery that my second wife, Cora, was having an affair with the man who came to clean our carpets—not the iceman, not the milkman, but the goddamn carpet man! Isn't that a frigging hoot? The situation had me on the precipice of another divorce.

"Give her a call," Marge said. "I know she would want to hear from you."

That was one of those junctures where my life might have changed for the better. I know I should have called Janie—I believe she would have seen me back then—but I didn't do it. I had begun to drink, and maybe I was ashamed of the mess I had made of my life. Perhaps I had an altruistic moment and didn't want to hurt her again. About two years later, I heard that she had remarried; so, I never called.

This morning when I awoke, even before I could clear the confused jumble of vodka-induced cobwebs from my brain, vague thoughts of someone I used to know floated around inside my head. By the time I got my old blue robe around me and slipped on my shoes, the amorphous uncertainty took form, and the face of a young Janie Taggard emerged.

"I still love you, Jimmy," the face said.

She was probably the only person, other than my sister, who ever truly loved me. For such a long time, that didn't matter. I didn't need her or anyone else, not even the two wives I married. They were all dispensable. Now, after nearly eighteen years, I find myself thinking of Janie and wondering how different my life might have been if I had married her. Could I have come to really love her, or would I have hurt her much more than I did many years ago?

Janie and I began dating in our junior year of high school. She was not beautiful, but she was a pretty girl and the best twirler on the band majorette squad. When she was in the eighth and ninth grades, she looked like a twig, but she began to fill out when she was a sophomore. It was the way she appeared in her majorette outfit that attracted me to her.

Janie had just shed her image as a skinny little waif; it was obvious that she had not yet developed confidence in her appearance. The idea that she was attractive to boys probably had not occurred to her. I believe she was thrilled and surprised when I asked her for a date. She told me she had liked me for a long time. After our second date, she said that she was in love with me. I had no idea what love was—not real, unselfish love—and I wasn't sure she did either. However, I know that by the time we were preparing for graduation, she loved me deeply, and I cared for her as much as I was capable of doing.

I wasn't looking for a long-term relationship with Janie. I had hoped for an easy conquest, but she let me know right away that she planned to remain a virgin until she was married. I had heard that from other girls and was not deterred in my efforts to seduce her. I considered her virginity a challenge to my manhood, and I was determined that I would eventually prevail, even if that required my telling her I was in love with her. I eventually grew bold enough to put my hand on her breast as we sat in the back row of the theater. She didn't speak and didn't push my hand away, but she looked at me sadly in a manner that made me ashamed of what I had done. I realized then that Janie was a special girl who really deserved my respect and as much love as I had to give.

Our families and friends assumed we would get married right after high school, but we decided to wait until after Janie graduated from college. She enrolled in the local junior college to start earning her degree as a schoolteacher. I volunteered for the Army.

The night before I was scheduled to leave for basic training, we went to the drive-in theater. I parked my car in the last row. We couldn't have cared less about the movie. That night we wanted to spend time alone. The theater gave us the privacy to be as intimate as Janie would allow herself to be. I held her close, and we kissed more passionately than we had ever kissed before. I cupped her breast in my hand; she didn't resist.

"I love you," she said, holding me tightly against her.

"I love you too, Janie."

After all the nights of frustration I had spent holding Janie, wanting to make love to her, it happened so quickly and so easily. I unbuttoned her blouse and caressed and kissed her naked breasts. She breathed warmly against my neck as I raised her dress and pulled her panties aside.

"No," she said, as I attempted to make love to her. "No, please don't."

"Do you really love me, Janie?"

"Yes, I do, but I can't."

"I won't see you for three months," I said. "I need you tonight."

"Please, let's wait until we're married."

"What does it matter?" I said. "We're getting married, aren't we?"

"Yes," she said, relaxing beneath me.

"I love you," I assured her.

I pushed against her. She pulled away slightly and whimpered momentarily in pain as I entered her. Gradually, she began to return my kisses and hold onto me desperately. Moments later, it was over. I moved away from her and watched in silence as she rearranged her clothing. Her eyes glistened, but no tears fell. She smiled weakly. "Let's go home now."

We drove home without speaking. Each time I looked in her direction, she turned away and stared out the window. I suppose she was ashamed to look at me.

"You know I did that for you, Jimmy." she finally said, with her face still turned toward the passenger window.

"Yes."

When I stopped the car in front of her house, she said, "Please don't get out."

She stood beside the car with the passenger door open. I was unable to see her face. I assumed she needed to be consoled, but I didn't know what to say to her. I suppose I could have told her effusively how much I loved her, but at that moment I would have been compounding matters with a terrible lie. Eventually, she bent over to look at me through the open door.

"I love you, Jimmy; I hope you will always remember that."

"I love you too, Janie," I said, but I was devoid of feeling. I realized she was suddenly aware that she had given her virginity to someone who did not love her nearly as much as she loved him. I know she was disappointed in herself, but I was disappointed in her too. She was no different than other girls I had known; she was not special. I had succeeded in pulling her off her pedestal, and I no longer respected her.

"I would never have done anything if I didn't love you," she said as if she understood what I was thinking.

I got out and went around to the other side of the car. I put my arm around her and walked with her to the front door. I kissed her gently and left her standing there. She gave a slight wave of her hand as I drove away.

While I was in boot camp, we exchanged letters two or three times each week, and I called her almost every weekend. In one of those letters, Janie told me she believed she was pregnant. She had not told anyone in her family, but she realized she would have to do it soon. I waited until the next weekend to call her. By then I had concluded that neither of us was ready for a baby and that I would ask her to end the pregnancy.

"Are you sure you're pregnant?" I asked.

"Yes, Jimmy, I am; my mother and I went to see the doctor Monday. There isn't any doubt."

"Damn," I said. "What rotten luck!"

"What do you mean?"

"I mean I am not ready for a kid."

I could hear her crying softly. "I can't believe you would say that under these circumstances."

"But what about your college?"

"Those plans will have to wait."

"They don't have to," I said.

Except for occasional weak sobs, she made no sounds. After several minutes, she said, sounding desperate, "Tell me what you want me to do."

"You have to get an abortion."

After a few more minutes of silence, she said, "Good-bye, Jimmy. Don't come to see me when you are home on leave."

"Wait, Janie," I said, but it was too late for her to hear me.

I considered calling her again to tell her I was sorry and that I would marry her now. However, on second thought, I told myself it would be better to let her think about things for a while.

Maybe she would decide that I was right after all. A few days later, I received a letter from Janie, letting me know that she would have the baby without my support. I still have that letter. I read it four years ago right after my sister called me and again this morning.

> *Dear Jimmy,*
>
> *I love you—no, that is not what I want to say. What I want to say is that I love the person you could be, but not the person you have become. I suppose I will always love the boy who asked me for a date and made me feel special for the first time in my life. Unfortunately, that boy did not become the man I want to marry or the father I want for my child.*
>
> *I am freeing you of responsibility for my condition. I will do whatever I must to have this baby, and I will nurture it with all my heart. I will do so without any help from you. The baby will never know you. And that will be your loss.*
>
> *There will always be a place for you in my heart. That place has been diminished, but it will always be there. How can it not?*
>
> *Goodbye,*
> *Janie*

I was surprised by the frankness of her letter and was touched by the hurt she expressed. She had revealed strengths that I was unaware she possessed. Nevertheless, nothing she could have said would have made me want to accept the responsibilities of being a father at nineteen. Janie's letter had given me a way out. Although I didn't feel very good about myself, at least I was free of the shackles marriage and children would have imposed at such a young age. If Janie was willing to accept responsibility for her situation, I was willing to let her do it.

My sister remained in touch with Janie over the years. When the baby was born, Marge called to tell me that I was the father of a little girl. Marge emphasized that Janie did not want me to contact her. The child was later adopted by Janie's first husband, and she doesn't know that I exist. She will never know me unless Janie decides to tell her someday.

Conventional wisdom says that we eventually pay for our sins. The knowledge that we are failures, that we could have been better than we are and that we are not worthy of the love of others should be recompense enough. However, conventional wisdom does not apply to me. There is nothing I can do to assuage my sins.

The young face of Janie Taggard will fade away when I drown her image in vodka and wine. Perhaps if I drink enough, I will never again experience the pleasures and pain that remembering Janie brings. Until that happens, I will imagine how different my life might have been with her. What if I had rushed home and married her when she informed me she was pregnant? What if I had called her four years ago? Would I now know the joys of having a loving wife? Would my seventeen-year-old daughter put her arms around me and tell me that she loves me?

What if I had taken a different road? Would that have changed my life, or would I still suffer the same self-imposed travails?

Fairy Tales

W ho was that man?" Jonathan asked. He looked up from his plate toward his mother, and then glanced at me. It was as if he had been waiting all afternoon to ask the question that would quiet a nagging suspicion something was not right between Mommy and Daddy. Jonathan was precocious at nine years of age.

I looked across the table at Sarah. She raised both eyebrows, shrugging her shoulders as her lips closed around a spoonful of potatoes and corn. I can't imagine what he's talking about, I took her gesture to mean.

I laid my knife and fork across my plate and slid my chair back from the table. Perhaps I could answer his question. "What man, Jonathan?"

"The man at the motel."

"He's Mommy's friend," seven-year-old Jennifer said before I could speak. She was happy she knew the answer to something Jonathan did not.

Sarah wasn't talking. She chewed her food deliberately and avoided my eyes.

"Which friend?" I asked, placing my hand on Jennifer's small fingers.

"Mommy's friend—you know, Daddy." She pulled her hand away from mine and began to eat again, as if she had put the matter to rest once and for all.

"You want to jump in here?" I asked Sarah. I was irritated that she had not said anything to clear up the matter, which was obviously making both of us uncomfortable.

Sarah replied, "She means the new pastor. I told you that Pastor Barlow and his wife are staying at the Hampton Inn until the rectory is ready. I dropped some pictures off there."

"Wasn't Pastor Barlow," Jonathan said, "was somebody else."

Sarah didn't blink an eye.

Jonathan seemed compelled to continue talking. "Jenny and I stayed in the van."

I glowered at Sarah, searching her face for an explanation. I wondered what story she was fabricating behind her beauty queen facade. She used her knife to cut the piece of chicken on her plate. She took a bite and chewed methodically. I imagined the chicken turning to sawdust in her mouth as she realized I probably would not believe whatever she had to say.

Jonathan continued, "While Mommy was in the motel room, we watched Snow White on the DVD."

"All of it?" I asked, realizing there was a hell of a lot more to the motel story than Sarah wanted me to know.

"No, just the first part, but I hate that movie. I'm too old for it."

"Then why did you watch it?" I asked.

"'Cause crybaby Jenny wanted to."

Sarah sat stoically. She had perfected a disinterested pose even while a noose was tightening around her neck.

I reminded myself that the dinner table was not the place for an inquisition. Any further discussion would yield only consummate lies from Sarah and accusations from me. I wanted an end to the matter until after the children were asleep in bed.

"It's OK, Jonathan," I lied. "Mother told me before I went to work this morning she was going to the Hampton Inn today … didn't you, Mother?"

"Uh-huh," Sarah said, nodding her head affirmatively.

"Wasn't the Hampton Inn," Jonathan said. "It was Ramada."

Sarah never changed the expression on her face. She calmly reached for the bowl of mashed potatoes and emptied a spoonful onto her plate, but I knew her mind was going ninety miles an hour trying to think of some plausible explanation for her misstep. She had forgotten that children grow up quickly; they talk, they ask questions, and they want logical answers. I had grown up also—perhaps wiser but certainly many years older than when I sat down to the meal.

I stood and placed my napkin alongside my plate. "Do you have another explanation, Sarah?"

"If I can think of one, I will tell you," she said, stabbing the piece of chicken on her plate with her fork.

"Well, when you do, make certain it's believable. Jonathan and I are too old for fairy tales."

Hill Top Motel

The Hill Top Motel has been their meeting place for the past ten years. For one day in September of each year, Taylor and Rebecca share the remembrance of their first kiss nearly twenty years ago. They rekindle passions neither will ever experience with anyone else. When the day is over, they say good-bye, savoring quiet exhilaration and accepting lingering guilt.

A few hours each year is so little to give each other, but it is much to take from the ones to whom they are bound and have promised everything. With each "I love you," they are reminded that these same words were said only a few hours earlier to the others for whom they care. They speak of things that might have been but never will be. On parting, each expects nothing more from the other than to be remembered often.

Today, Taylor has made all the arrangements for their reunion. He waits patiently for the next two hours to pass. Then he will hear Rebecca's soft knock on the door. She will enter after quickly looking around to ascertain that she has not been followed; he smiles at the thought that Rebecca will never change. Once she is inside, he will kiss her fervently before asking, "Are you OK?" And before she can answer, he will say, "You are as beautiful as ever."

For several weeks, he has anticipated seeing Rebecca again. Following his arrival yesterday, he slept fitfully and woke early. After breakfast, he went for a walk. He bought a bottle of wine and a single yellow rose, her favorite flower. Now, alone in the room, he waits impatiently to hold her. He turns on the television and lies back on a pillow to watch. Moments later, he is lost in reverie, recalling too many poignant moments to keep in perspective. Scenes and words, over which he has little control, traverse his mind.

"Be careful," Rebecca said. "You'll get grass stains on my dress; how will I explain that to Mother?"

They had spread a blanket on the grassy knoll above the B&O Railway station. Rebecca lay looking up into Taylor's eyes. He would be leaving the next morning for Navy basic training.

"Don't worry," he said. "I won't get you in trouble with your mother, not now or ever. I love you too much for that."

There, near the park bench overlooking the train yard, where he first kissed her, they spent their last hour together talking of their future, her forthcoming birthday, and Taylor's plan to give her an engagement ring for Christmas. He was eighteen and Rebecca just sixteen. Four months apart would be their longest separation since they met nearly two years earlier. However, four months would prove to be much too long. By the time he arrived home on leave, Rebecca would have fallen in love with someone else. She planned to marry David that summer, after her high school graduation.

She had kept her new love interest a secret from Taylor as long as possible. When he called from home to say he was on his way to see her, she made her revelation.

"There's something I have to tell you."

"And I have lots to tell you too."

"No, seriously." Her words faltered, and Taylor's heart sank as she continued, "There's someone else."

After a moment, he regained enough composure to ask, "How long have you known?"

"A little while."

"And that's it? It's over without seeing me?"

"It won't help. You can't change my mind."

"It'll help me," he said. "I need to see you."

Taylor drove impatiently across town. There were far too many traffic lights along his route, and they stayed red much longer than usual. The cars in front of him crept along, their drivers deliberately keeping him from reaching Becky. He knew that if he could hold her one more time, she would know she still loved him. But when he finally looked into her face, he realized things were not as they had been that night before he went away. They talked across the backyard fence where she had come to explain her plans to marry David.

"It just happened," she said.

"You said you loved me."

"I believed I did."

"What did I do to make you change your mind?"

"Nothing. You'd just have to know David to understand."

"I don't want to know David."

"Don't you want to know anything about him?"

"No, I want to know why you didn't wait; that's all."

"I was fourteen when we met. You were the first boy I ever kissed. I guess I didn't really know what love was."

"You could have let me know."

"I didn't know how to tell you."

"The way you're telling me now, Becky."

"I didn't want to hurt you."

"But you did—"

"I'm sorry, Taylor," she interrupted.

"More than you know," he continued.

"I'm sorry, Taylor. I really am."

She touched his arm gently. He looked into her eyes and saw her unspoken plea for understanding. He wanted to hold and comfort her. He touched her hair across the fence and then kissed her sweetly on the cheek. He said, "If you ever need me, Becky, ever, let me know."

Taylor's Navy service took him far away from Rebecca. He wanted desperately to be in love with someone else, yet he relished his thoughts of her. He met other girls, but none of them could make him forget Becky; he knew he would love her forever. At twenty, he married someone he had known only a few weeks. They divorced a year later.

At the end of his three-year Navy enlistment, he took a job with a naval architectural company. After three years, he was promoted to a senior management position. During his infrequent visits home, he was continually reminded of Rebecca. It had been nearly five years since their breakup, but he was still not over her; he thought he might never be. Once, he drove to her street and passed by her house several times, hoping to catch a glimpse of her. Afterward, he realized that his obsession with Rebecca had to end.

Taylor devoted himself to his job as never before. There were no vacations, no free weekends, and no hobbies outside his work. He was soon promoted to vice president of the company. He married his secretary, Janice, and became a father six months later. His wife was a beautiful young woman with interests much in common with Taylor's. He was content with his life and his thoughts of Rebecca were subdued and less frequent. However, that would change when he made his next trip back to his hometown.

It had been nearly eight years since he stood at Rebecca's backyard fence telling her goodbye. Now she had two boys, ages three and five. She was a devoted mother and wife, but Taylor would learn that she had doubts of her own and fond memories she could not ignore. For her, sex with David had been a great disappointment; she often wondered how it might have been with Taylor. She was oblivious to any thought that she soon would reveal these innermost secrets at the Hill Top Motel.

On his way from the airport, Taylor drove by the old B&O Railway station. At the top of the hill, he parked for a moment and looked down the sloping ground where he had lain on the grass with Rebecca so many years before. Once again, he heard her words of love and promise. At that moment, he realized his efforts at getting over her had failed. He could no longer deny his feelings: he loved Becky and had to see her.

So many times, he had picked up the phone with the intention of calling, but he always decided against it. This time, he dialed the number and waited nervously.

"Hello."

"Mrs. Miller, please," he said very formally.

"This is she."

"Rebecca?"

"Yes?"

"Taylor," he said.

"Oh, my God!"

"How are you?"

"I'm well. How about you?"

"OK. Missing you still after all these years."

She was silent.

"Are you happy, Becky?"

"I guess so. David is a wonderful husband."

"I don't doubt that. Janice is wonderful too, but are you happy?"

"I have two boys to consider."

"And I have a daughter, but that doesn't stop me from loving you."

"Please, don't say that."

"I have to say it. That's why I called."

For several seconds, neither spoke. Taylor realized they were at a tipping point in their lives, and each was choosing words carefully.

"I'm almost afraid to say this to you because so many lives are at stake," she said, "but I think of you so often. I've had these thoughts all these years. I know I shouldn't, but I do."

His heart pounded as his mind raced to comprehend. *Becky loved him. Becky wanted to see him.* At that moment, nothing else mattered. He was prepared to accept any and all consequences. He would make love to her, and both would have to live with their sins. But nothing could be worse than the torment of the past eight years.

"I have wanted to see you, but I didn't know how you felt about it," he said. "I've even driven by your house hoping to see you."

"You really are crazy about me, aren't you?" she joked.

"I guess I'm crazy in love with you."

"I knew my feelings couldn't be one-way," she said. "I have thought about you so much and wanted to see you. I knew you still loved me."

They met the next day at the downtown mall. She waited by the main entrance. He recognized her immediately and thought she had not changed at all. Taylor pulled the car alongside the curb and motioned for her to get in. She closed the door after herself and fastened the seat belt. As he drove away from the mall, she diverted her eyes from his glances.

"Where are we going?"

"I have a room."

"My stomach is fluttering," she said, "I don't know how to handle this."

"It's OK," he said, "You don't have to do anything you don't want to do."

"And what do you want me to do?"

"I want to make love to you."

Alone in the room, they kissed. Taylor opened wine and they drank a toast to their reunion. After more wine and talk of things that had gone unsaid between them for too long, he slowly removed her clothing. That afternoon, they loved each other unselfishly.

"Are you sorry we never made love when we were young?" she asked, lying in his arms.

"No. It only makes today more special."

"You know I love my husband."

"I'm sure you do, but I know you love me too."

"How do you love two people at the same time?" she asked.

"In different ways," he said. "We love many people but in different ways."

"How do you love me?"

"Like no one else in the world."

"And how do I love you?"

"You love me the same way I love you … else you wouldn't be here."

"How do you know me so well?"

"Because I never forgot, Becky."

They watched the afternoon tick away minute by minute, hoping that time would suddenly stand still for just a little while. They knew their day would come to an end much too soon and that they would have to face the consequences of separation and guilt.

"I have to be home when the boys get off their school bus," she said.

"And I have a plane to catch this evening."

He held her hand as he drove to the mall parking lot. Their euphoria had turned to sadness with the reality that it probably would be a long time before they could see each other again.

"Please don't think poorly of me for what I've done," she said sadly, as she opened the car door to get out.

"How could I when I love you so much?"

"Don't stop loving me, Taylor. I won't be able to bear it if you ever do, not after what we have done today."

"I have needed to stop loving you so many times in the past, but I never could," he said, "So don't worry. I won't ever stop."

That September day ended like many others to come during the next nine years. Occasionally, when he was in town, he met Rebecca for a quick lunch or a walk in the park. Phone calls between them were infrequent and took place only on very special occasions, but the month of September was to be remembered and celebrated. It was the month of their first kiss and the month when they finally consummated their love. It would become the month during which they met every year to give themselves to each other.

Now, Taylor waited for Becky to arrive, just as he had done so many times. He looked at the clock and realized he must have fallen asleep for an hour; it was almost one in the afternoon. She was late. His imagination conjured unlikely reasons why she had not come to the room on time or had not called. Moments later, the phone rang. He sat up on the side of the bed and answered it.

"Hello."

"Hi," she said.

"What's wrong? Why are you so late?"

He heard her subdued sobbing. "What has happened, Rebecca?"

"I can't see you, Taylor."

"Why? Does David know about us?"

"No. No …. I just can't do this anymore."

"What do you mean?"

"I've been thinking … feeling more guilt than usual; I guess I'm just getting too old to do this."

He listened quietly as she continued. "We aren't kids any longer, but we try to act is if we still are. We are taking awful chances that we will hurt someone else, especially our children and for what purpose?"

"We love each other, Rebecca. We don't ask for much for ourselves."

"What good does it do for us to see each other one day each year? At the end of the day, you go your way, and I go mine, and what do we have left except heartbreak and guilt?"

"We have a very special love."

"It isn't enough anymore."

"That's the way you have always wanted it, Becky. I would have done anything you asked. I would have gotten a divorce. You know that."

"But I can't divorce David. It would break his heart. My children would hate me."

"I love you, Becky. I need to see you one more time, just today; then we will decide about the future."

"I can't do it. If I was there with you, I wouldn't have the courage to tell you these things."

"Let me see you one more time. You don't have to come here. I will meet you at the mall."

"I can't. It has taken all my willpower to call to tell you this. Please don't ask to see me, please. If I don't stand firm now, I will never be able to let you go, but I really need to, as much as you need to let me go."

He held back tears as he reflected on Rebecca's words. He smiled at how wise she had become since their first reunion ten years ago. She had looked to him for strength so often, but now it was obvious that she possessed the strength that would allow both to face reality.

"I understand," he said.

"I have to go before I cry again, Taylor."

"Are you sure?"

"No, I'm not sure, but I have to do this while I have the courage."

"I will miss you, Becky."

"I know," she said. "Please don't ever stop missing me."

"I don't do good-byes very well, but I will let you go."

"Good-bye."

"Good-bye, Becky."

Taylor turned off the television and lay across the bed, assessing his emotions. He was so proud of Becky at that moment, so much in love with her. He had never stood in her way or tried to direct her heart where she did not want it to go. If her decision was not to see him again, he would do his best to abide by it. He would go on with his life without her.

He got up from the bed and packed his bag in preparation for checkout. As he placed the final articles into the bag, the telephone rang. He knew instinctively it was Rebecca.

He listened without speaking. He heard her quiet sobs as she said, almost pleading, "Are you there, Taylor? Are you there?"

She continued to cry softly. As he listened, the urge to comfort her was almost irresistible, but he kept his silence. After a moment she said, "I love you, Taylor. I wish I could offer you more than that."

He was mindful of the courage she had shown and his own failure to be as courageous as she. She had summoned her inner strength to make a decision he should have made long ago. He thought of the terrible torment she must have endured with each secret tryst; he could not ask her to go through it again. Now, as she demurred in the most important decision of her life, he would not give her reason to go back. He knew with certainty she loved him, and the knowledge of her love would sustain him. He saw that his love for Rebecca had been selfish. He now understood that if he truly loved her, he would let her go.

He slowly replaced the phone in its cradle and picked up the bag near the bed. As the door to room two seventeen of the Hill Top Motel closed shut behind him, he never looked back.

One New Year's Eve

From my position in the living room, I noticed them through the kitchen archway. She stood with her back to the counter. He was close to her—close enough to require her to tilt her head upward to look into his face as they talked. I could see there was something going on between them, or at least about to be. The way she was looking at him was different than the way she ever looked at me now, maybe close to the way it was when we first met. The two of them seemed to be indifferent to my frequent glances in their direction.

My wife, Gloria, who obviously had had too much to drink, was talking to my good friend and fellow officer, Lieutenant John Shelly. We were stationed together on a naval destroyer based in Norfolk, Virginia. He lived on the first floor of a Navy housing project. Gloria and I lived on the second floor. John's wife was away visiting her parents for the holidays. He had invited my wife and me and several other friends to celebrate the new year. Our two young daughters were asleep upstairs.

Gloria and I had become good party people. We knew how to talk, smile, share drinks, tell quaint little jokes in mixed company, and of course pay compliments to the host and hostess, especially to senior officers and their wives. Gloria's mixing and mingling skills were very evident after a few too many drinks. I had observed my shipmate John in action often enough to understand that if presented with the opportunity, he knew how to take advantage of an intoxicated lady.

I should have made my way to my wife's side, unobtrusively taken her hand, and led her out of a dubious situation, or perhaps I could have dramatically defended my honor by delivering a knee to the groin of John Shelly, leaving him writhing in pain on his own kitchen floor, but I did neither. I had grown weary of protecting Gloria from herself. I pushed open the sliding glass door leading to the balcony, walked out on the deck, and lit up a cigarette. For several minutes I stood looking across the snow-covered parking lot and feeling the cold night air blow on my face. I wondered why in the hell I had attended John's party at all.

* * *

I didn't notice her standing next to me until I felt her arm against mine. I turned to look at her. She held a glass of white wine tentatively in her right hand and a long, slim cigarette between two fingers of the other. It was obvious she had disposed of several glasses of wine prior to the current one. I recognized her as Millie Gunter, the wife of another officer. Her husband, Gil, was also a lieutenant, the only black officer that I knew who was stationed onboard any of the destroyers at the Norfolk base. Millie was tall, bronzed, and nicely built—a very pretty woman. The one distraction from her attractive appearance was the horn-rimmed glasses that were much too large to suit her face.

Millie lived just across the parking lot, in an upstairs apartment. I had seen her occasionally in our building, visiting a girlfriend who lived on the ground floor. I had never spoken to her except to say hello a few times, so I was surprised at the manner in which she chose to start a conversation with me on that New Year's Eve.

"What's going on between Gloria and John?" she asked, motioning her head toward the two of them without looking in their direction.

"What do you mean?"

"I mean did you see them in the kitchen? You better watch out, Larry, you better—"

"Hell, they're just talking," I said, annoyed that Millie was voicing exactly what I had been thinking. "Nothing's going on."

Millie glanced at her watch and held her arm up in the light for me to see.

"Almost midnight, huh?"

"Yeah, almost."

We smoked our cigarettes without speaking again and flipped the butts onto the snow piled alongside the walkway below. Millie downed her drink, then, smiling triumphantly, held the glass upside down to show that it was empty. As the last minute of the old year wound down, I looked back at Gloria still standing near John. They touched glasses, and as shouts of "Happy New Year" erupted from behind the glass doors, she kissed him on the cheek. I watched her as she looked around, then moved through the other guests in apparent search for me.

Millie rested her elbows on the top banister. She was quiet. The broad smile had left her face, and tears moistened the corners of her eyes. I put my arm around her shoulder to comfort her. She turned toward me, looking vulnerable and inviting. I kissed her gently on the mouth.

"Happy New Year, Millie," I said, as I looked into her dark eyes.

She pulled away, giving me a glance that told me she had known from the start I was going to kiss her and that she was not entirely unhappy it had happened. She turned toward the living room.

"Wait, Millie," I said. "I'm sorry."

"Happy New Year, Larry," she said, without looking back.

"Happy New Year," I said, hoping that Millie would not make more of the kiss than I had intended. I lit another cigarette and smoked it as I listened to the celebratory cacophony from various sections of our apartment compound.

* * *

"Having a good time?" Gloria asked over my shoulder.

"Wonderful," I replied, turning around to look at her.

She walked over to me, put her face against my cheek, and kissed me. "Happy New Year, honey."

"I wasn't sure you knew I was still here."

"Don't be jealous," she teased. "John and I were just talking; he's so funny."

"Yeah, he has me in stitches right now," I said. "I ought to kick his ass or yours; I just haven't figured out which one."

"Don't be silly, Larry; don't spoil the party."

"Sure," I said, "go on, party. But I think I'm through celebrating for the night."

"You're gonna catch yourself a cold," she said, and then paused for several seconds. "Do me a favor?"

"Sure," I said. "What? Drop dead?"

Gloria laughed.

"Millie has had too much to drink, and the parking lot is frozen. Help her walk home. Make sure she's OK before you leave her alone."

"I don't think that is such a good idea," I said, "Where's her husband?"

"Out celebrating the new year, the son of a bitch."

"Wow, and I was feeling sorry for myself."

Moments later I was holding Millie's arm as we walked across the parking lot and up the stairs to her apartment. She grasped my shoulder unsteadily as I fumbled with the key and finally opened the door. Once inside, I led her directly to the bedroom door and pushed it open. "Are you going to be alright?"

"I believe so," she said, "but give me a few minutes to make sure."

I sat on the sofa and waited. Millie emerged from the bedroom wearing her nightgown and robe.

"I'd better go," I said, well aware of the impropriety of the situation.

"Stay for a minute; I need someone to talk to." She sat beside me on the sofa. "What do you think about a man who leaves his wife to go celebrate on New Year's Eve?"

"I don't know what to say about that, Millie."

Although I believed it inconsiderate of Gil, I didn't know him or Millie well enough to offer advice about their relationship, especially since Gloria and I had problems of our own for which we had no ready solution.

She continued, "I can't understand why Gloria would go after John when she has you for a husband."

"You've got her wrong," I insisted.

"Think so?" she asked knowingly. "And where in the hell is my husband tonight?"

"Millie, if you're OK, I've got to leave," I said, not wanting to discuss Gil's probable philandering or my wife's very obvious overtures to my downstairs friend and neighbor.

Millie stood. She loosened her sash and pulled open her robe, revealing two long, shapely legs. Her short white nightgown contrasted with her light brown skin. Without her glasses, she was beautiful and alluring. "See what Gil left at home tonight? Not bad, huh?"

"You're gorgeous, Millie," I said. "Gil must be a fool." I got up from the sofa to leave.

She stood on her toes, raised her face to mine, and kissed me. For the moment, I returned her kiss without embracing her. She shrugged the robe off her shoulders, letting it fall down her back. I pulled her close to me as our bodies sank together onto the sofa.

"You and I are asking for a lot of trouble," I said, looking down at her.

"I know, but I don't care," she said. "Not tonight."

* * *

It was almost one thirty in the morning. Gloria was asleep in our bed. I looked into our little girls' room; they were sleeping peacefully. I tucked the covers around them and returned to our bedroom. As I undressed, Gloria roused from her sleep.

"Where've you been?"

"At Millie's," I said. "We talked."

"She OK?"

"Yes, but I can't understand that husband of hers. Why would he leave her alone tonight of all nights?"

"I know," Gloria mused. "Isn't it strange?"

"It is strange."

"Well, everyone can't have a marriage as perfect as ours, can they now?" she said, as she pulled the covers up around her face.

"I guess not," I said. "Going back to sleep?"

"Yes," she said. "Happy New Year."

My Life as a Cowboy

When a man gets into his forties, he can begin to think life is passing him by, so he decides he has to change things. It happened to me when I was forty-two. I just couldn't stand my situation any longer. A man's wife no longer *understands* him when he reaches forty-two, and of course he needs a new spouse, so I got me one. Lenora was a beauty of a Southern belle with a pronounced Mississippi drawl. Honey dripped from her mouth, and I licked it up. It was only natural that, with such inspiration and my renewed youthful vigor, I would get her pregnant—I did. We married one week after my divorce and four months before our son was born.

We bought a four-bedroom, three-bath stucco ranch home, which we both fell in love with as soon as we saw it. Two months after moving in, Lenora grew tired of the house, so she hired a contractor and an interior decorator to change everything. The contractor took out a couple of walls and added a new one. The decorator installed new wainscoting, new wallpaper, new curtains, new furniture, and new appliances to match. As soon as that was done, Lenora just had to have the back deck and patio enlarged, which projects were completed two weeks before the inground pool was started. My business was going well, so paying for all the things, including the new Lincoln Town Car, required to keep Lenora occupied and content was not a massive problem.

And she was happy coping with her hectic schedule of talking on the phone, visiting her girlfriends, overseeing the cleaning lady, supervising the day-time sitter who cared for our new son, Jason, and occasionally preparing dinner. It was about a year before she decided she wanted horses. Oh, yes, I almost forgot—she also learned that she was pregnant again. Seven months later we had a baby named Juliet.

Live Oaks's sixty acres of fenced and cross-fenced land came complete with pond, tractor, wagon, and forty-seven head of Black Angus cattle, including a ferocious- looking black bull with big balls. At a price of $450,000, the property was a bargain, especially when I considered how happy the thought of living in the country made my beautiful young wife. Deciding to leave the little Mississippi city of Pascagoula, I took out a bigger mortgage and bought the country home. As we now had a farm with cows, I was an official cowboy. The horses would come later.

The first thing I learned after moving out into the country was that I had added a full hour to my work commute. That meant I had to get up at five thirty in the morning to have time for my morning feeding chores. I won't need to explain that the evening chores required another half hour of my time when I arrived home from the office around seven at night. My weekends were spent mending fences, hauling feed and supplies from the co-op (which task required the purchase of a $56,000, one-ton, dual-wheeled Dodge truck), disking fields, and planting millet or winter ryegrass. I was so exhausted at the end of the day, that things soon went to hell in the bedroom. It wasn't long before my pretty wife began to complain I never had time for her.

Remember the house with the enlarged back deck and patio—the one with the swimming pool? Well the farmhouse required a similar makeover. In came the interior decorator with her new wallpaper, drapes, furniture, and wall art, all coordinated, of course; but thank God no walls came down and no new ones went up. We did have to get an inground swimming pool, however, identical to the one we had given up just one year earlier.

I went about the business of learning to be a cattle baron with the same vigor and dedication I applied to anything I ever did. I was determined to learn all I could about raising cattle and perhaps even derive a little extra income from it. I bought myself some pointy-toed boots, a pair of cowboy-cut jeans, and a belt with a humongous silver buckle decorated with the image of a cowboy riding a bucking bronco. The crowning affirmation came when my ten-gallon hat arrived from the mail order store. I promptly settled my $135 purchase on my head, right down to my ears, and began to walk with a definite bowlegged Texas swagger.

While I was attending to the cattle ranch and overseeing my business in town, my pretty wife was buying horses. Before I even knew it, we had paid $26,000 for the privilege of owning three registered quarter horses and a champion pony. The animals were boarded at a horse ranch about ten miles away. It cost another $19,000 for saddles, tack, and a four-horse trailer, complete with dressing room. The latter purchase meant I lost the use of my Dodge truck, which was now used to pull the trailer. The cost of board, and the fact that I never saw my wife until bedtime each night, prompted me to get busy building a barn, which was completed at a cost of almost $55,000. Having the horses nearby at least eliminated her excuse for being away from home so much, and I got a chance to speak to her occasionally when I wasn't working or playing cowboy. It also meant that I could add to my evening and weekend chores the job of mucking out stalls when Lenora was not feeling well.

Managing a miniature ranch was not all bad. It has always been my philosophy that every experience is a good experience if you learn something from it, and I did learn from this episode in my life. I discovered much about breeding and feeding cows. I honed my veterinary skills learning how to pull a calf out of a cow's thingie when her water broke, leaving her baby's hooves exposed and dry. I found out that I was in for a hell of a lot of trouble when an unborn calf got turned upside down, its feet sticking out the cow's rear end and just hanging there, seemingly lifeless. I spent many a night sleeping in my pickup truck parked in one of the pastures so I could be close to a cow that was having trouble birthing. I became expert at locking the steers' heads in a headgate, then piercing their ears to attach fly tags or ramming a plastic tube down their throats to inject worming goo.

There were some things I just never got the hang of though. For example, I never did learn how you can tell when a cow is unhappy with her surroundings. She is like a woman in that respect—she just won't tell you. You only know she is unhappy after she has jumped a fence to get to greener pastures (just like a woman) or broken through the fence, taking half the herd with her. When that happens, it usually isn't much of a problem to round them up and get them all back in their pasture, except for the bull.

A bull does whatever the hell he wants to do, and one day my big-balled bull decided he did not wish to be confined to the sixty acres he reigned over on my side of the fence. I quickly discovered how to reclaim him when he escaped to unrestrained freedom on the adjoining property. After he chased me around a tree two or three times, I climbed on my tractor and pushed him through the hole in the fence. With a whoop, a holler, and a slap on his butt, I sent the bull romping at a gallop (Do bulls gallop?) toward the middle of the pasture. I then turned my attention to mending the fence.

I didn't know the bull was going to take the whole incident personally. I saw him saunter nonchalantly in my direction, but I neglected to realize he was still mulling over the terrible indignity I had foisted upon him. Just as I knelt down to stretch the lower strand of barbed wire, he rushed at me from behind. I heard him coming, and I rolled under the barbed wire to escape, but not before his right hoof broke three ribs and ruptured my spleen. I am certain I saw him sneer at me as I lay writhing in pain on the ground. While I was recuperating in hospital, Lenora hired a ranch hand to take care of the cows and to help with the horses and barn. She said his skill merited the $1,200 we paid him weekly.

In the hospital, I did some thinking about the way my life was turning out. I was almost fifty and not getting any younger. Hellfire, I was killing myself taking care of those cows, and for what? Ego? Status? Whatever it was, it wasn't worth it. I decided to get rid of the cows. I would sell them, build a larger barn, buy some more horses, and go into the quarter horse business big-time with Lenora. We could spend more time together, riding, training, and breeding horses; I knew that would make her happy.

When I returned home after three weeks, I was introduced to Chigger Burns, a six-foot two-inch, brawny, blond buckaroo, no better looking than Brad Pitt. He was one hell of a ranch hand, and it was easy to see why Lenora had such a high opinion of his skills. He could round up the cattle effortlessly and sit the saddle as well as anyone I had ever seen on the Saturday matinee when I was a kid. I decided to keep him on even after I recovered sufficiently to lift a bale of hay for the cows or carry feed buckets for the horses. I went ahead with my plans to sell the cows and called in a builder, with the intent of building another horse barn, this one to have eight boarding stalls, a washing stall, a tack room, and an adjoining enclosed paddock.

My pretty wife was happy, I was able to devote my attention to my faltering business, the cows were gone, and the horses were well attended to by Chigger Burns. I was no longer a cattle cowboy but now a quarter horse cowboy-rancher-magnate (a much more sophisticated kind of cowboy).

I was getting my life back on track. My business was recovering from three years of my inattention. We were beginning to break even (largely by taking advantage of tax write-offs) in the quarter horse business. All seemed well. That was when I got the call from my lawyer.

"She's served you," he said.

"What the hell do you mean?" I asked, not daring to try to decipher what I had just heard.

"I mean she has sued your dumb ass for divorce," my attorney said.

I stared silently into space, prompting my secretary to ask, "Mr. Rayborn, what's wrong?"

"Nothing. Just go on; we'll get back to this later. Close the door."

I turned my attention back to the attorney. "What are you saying, John? She's filed for divorce?"

"That's right—irreconcilable differences."

"What's she asking for?"

"Everything—the ranch, the kids, separate maintenance, alimony."

I am now living in a room in back of my office. Lenora and Chigger Burns are running a quarter horse ranch in the country. Oh, yes—they spend every other weekend in the three-bedroom condominium I used to own on the Redneck Riviera in Orange Beach, Alabama. And my ribs still ache when it rains.